MELINDA

MELINDA

Mildred J. Bartelt

*For Julia
with thanks
Mildred J Bartelt*

VANTAGE PRESS
New York

11/10/2006

This is a work of fiction. Any similarity between the names
and characters in this book and any real persons,
living or dead, is purely coincidental.

Cover design by Polly McQuillen

FIRST EDITION

Copyright © 2006 by Mildred J. Bartelt

Published by Vantage Press, Inc.
419 Park Ave. South, New York, NY 10016

Manufactured in the United States of America
ISBN: 0-533-15438-3

Library of Congress Catalog Card No.: 2006920034

0 9 8 7 6 5 4 3 2 1

To Dr. Susanne Abbott

MELINDA

1

Melinda

The cab slid to a stop opposite the dark alley and Rose flung open the door and pushed the two small children onto the sidewalk.

"Tell your grandma I'll pick you up. Sometime tomorrow." Rose giggled and squeezed the leg of the sailor sitting next to her.

"Maybe it won't be till Monday if I'm lucky. Stop sniveling, Richard, take Melinda's hand and before you know it, you'll be back to sleep in Grandma's crib."

Melinda grabbed Richard's limp pudgy hand and pulled the sleepy two-year-old near the building. She hated it when her mother did this so late at night. The alley was so dark and smelly. The walk to Grandma's house at the far end seemed twenty times as far as it did in the daytime. It wasn't so bad when Rose did this early in the evening when there were people walking down Queen Street, but it must now be around midnight and everything was quiet. Melinda was always scared that one of the bums who haunted the nearby bars during the day might be sleeping in the alley.

One night she had tripped over a sleeping drunk and he'd chased both of the children, cursing all the way.

Richard had slipped down onto the sidewalk and was prepared to drift off to sleep again. Melinda pulled hard on his arm.

"Get up, we've got to go down the alley before you can

1

go back to sleep. I know you are sleepy. I'm sleepy, too. It isn't fair for Mom to wake us up and send us off in the middle of the night, but you know she always tells us that it's the only way she can pay for our house and food." Melinda started to pull Richard into the alley.

The first ten feet or so were still lighted dimly from the street and soon it began to get pitch black. The four-story buildings on either side of the narrow alley blocked off any light from above.

The darker it got, the more Richard wailed and clung to Melinda's hand and skirt. Melinda felt her heart thump hard against her four-year-old chest. She felt tears begin to slide down her cheeks as she struggled with the desire to scream. Her feet went slower and slower, and the end of the alley seemed to always stay in the same place, no matter how many steps she took.

The uncovered trash cans which lined the alley smelled badly. This was Saturday. The whole week's malodorous, nauseating smells lay baking in the summer heat. With her free hand, Melinda covered her nose. This made it impossible to wave it from side to side to determine whether anything lay ahead of her, however, the stench was so horrible she had to do something to survive the two-hundred-foot ordeal.

The small pudgy hand slipped from her grasp suddenly as Richard sank to the ground and bellowed louder. Taking her hand from her nose Melinda swung both hands around in a circle near the ground, trying to find her wailing brother.

"Stop screaming, Richard," she whispered, "I can just see Grandma's porch light around the corner of the alley. Please get up. It won't be long now and then you can go back to sleep. I know it's scary and dark. Please be good for just a little while longer."

Melinda felt the tears beginning to course down her cheeks and she bit her lip. Anger at her mother surfaced along with the sinking feeling she always had when she had to deal with Richard on her own. Finally she managed to feel him several steps behind her and dragged him upright. He was getting so heavy it was impossible to pick him up, so she grabbed the back of his shirt and started pulling.

This only made Richard squirm and protest even louder. It was a good thing there weren't any of the sleeping bums around or by now they surely would have been awakened. At the insistence of her tugging, Richard once more got to his feet and lumbered after her. Once Melinda could see the porch light she felt comforted and managed to quicken her steps now that the goal was becoming visible. It still seemed a long time until she climbed the steps to the rickety porch and knocked on the door.

Richard's ruckus must have alerted Grandma, for the door opened almost immediately.

"Gracious, children, it's way past midnight!" She beckoned them into the cozy, well-worn, small front room.

"What's your ma doin' sending you out at this time of night? This is the third time this week. She must have found herself a live one with money. Come here Richard, you can stop crying. Grandma will fix you a glass of warm milk and you can go to sleep in your dad's room."

Dolores Dixon picked up her crying grandchild and comforted him as she carried him into the kitchen.

Dolores was weary of taking care of the little ones at no notice and at all hours, but she never let them know that they weren't anything but welcome. After all, the poor children didn't realize that their mother had turned into a prostitute. Rose knew that Dolores wouldn't shut the door on the children and that when she came back for them Dolores wouldn't make a fuss. She didn't want the children to hear the kind of language it would take to register her indignation at all that Rose was putting them through.

Frequently, when Rose returned, Dolores had asked that the children be allowed to stay with her until Douglas would be sent home from his tour of duty. Rose always refused, saying flatly that the children should be with their mother. The truth probably was that she wouldn't be getting her allotment check or the supplemental welfare money if she didn't have the children, and Dolores knew it.

Melinda followed her grandma into the small kitchen and watched while she put milk on the stove to heat. She didn't particularly like warm milk, but since there hadn't been any milk at home for several days, she looked forward to the bedtime treat. She wiped her eyes with the tail of her shirt and put her head down on the scrubbed oilcloth-covered table. It was always like this. Richard got all the attention. Grandma didn't seem to notice that she was crying and the trip down the alley in the dark had been so scary. Her shoulders started to shake convulsively and she felt herself slipping off the edge of the chair.

When Dolores turned from the stove with the two hot cups of milk, she noticed Melinda on the floor.

"Guess she's all tuckered out. Just isn't fair. Just isn't fair. Here, Richard, drink your milk while I put your sister on the couch."

As she picked Melinda up, she noticed that she was very cold and hardly weighed as much as Richard. She couldn't help but wonder how well the child was eating. If she guessed right, Melinda was probably letting Richard hog down all the food and eating the leftovers. Dolores knew this grandchild who was shy and withdrawn would never let on what was happening. Some inner loyalty to her mother made Melinda close-mouthed. That Melinda missed her dad was obvious from the few remarks she made when they had looked over the family picture album. Aside from that, she never complained. Dolores lay her gently on the

4

couch. No need for a blanket, it was hot despite the open windows in the back. She couldn't keep the front windows open because of the stench from the alley. Melinda curled into a ball.

When Dolores and Allen had bought the house forty-two years ago, there wasn't a tall building on Queen Street. The dirt path that led to the house made living in the middle of a field seem nice. Downtown was still several blocks away then, but gradually the town had started to grow and before you knew it there was a row of stores with apartments above them facing the front of their house. The dirt path was now the alley, which was the only way you could get from their house to the street. Once, twenty years before when the buildings that faced the back of her house were built, a contractor had offered them a thousand dollars to move out. They wanted to tear down the house and use the space for a parking lot.

Allen and Dolores had tried to find another house, however real estate was booming following the erection of the plastics plant. Doug was doing so well in school that they wanted to save to send him to college. They decided to stay where they were. It was a good thing too, since Allen began to get sick shortly after and could only work part time. They had managed to send Douglas to college. Dolores was proud of that.

After she put Richard in Douglas' room upstairs, Dolores settled down in the front bedroom. A small fan circulated air to her room, which wasn't the coolest but somehow she couldn't bring herself to move into Douglas' room. She couldn't get to sleep. There must be some way she could get Douglas home. Now that Allen was dead she didn't have anyone close with whom she could share such a terrible burden. She could just hear her sister Tilly, if she told her what her daughter-in-law was doing and how she was having to care for the grandchildren while Rose had her "fun" with any and everyone.

She certainly wasn't about to write Douglas and have him worry about the kids. She loved them dearly, and doted on them both. It would be bad enough for him to find out about Rose when he got home. The clock struck two before Dolores drifted off into a fitful sleep, filled with dreams of being alone in a house with many rooms but with children in every one. At six, a small hand on her cheek wakened her.

"I'm hungry," Richard said, as he stood, looking pitiful, beside the bed.

"Come on then," Dolores said, as she slipped on a robe and slippers and took him by the hand. "Let's see if there's any more of that special cereal you asked me to buy. Be careful on these steps and hold onto the banister."

Melinda was still sleeping on the couch and Dolores put her finger on her lips, signaling Richard to be quiet and not wake his sister. Once she had placed a bowl of cereal in front of him she knew he'd be quiet. Warming up the coffee left over from the previous evening and making toast for both of them consumed the next few minutes.

It was amazing to watch this small boy stuff his mouth full of food and without asking, push his bowl over for a refill. It was obvious that he had been eating, for he was a roly-poly. Dolores suspected that what he'd been eating was junk food because she knew that even though Rose had an electric stove she wasn't cooking anything much.

In a way she felt sorry for Rose. She had been much too young when Douglas married her. She had been a freshman when Douglas was a senior at Columbia. Then right away she had gotten pregnant and had to drop out of school and move to Dimsdale. Allen had objected because Rose wasn't a Catholic, but Doug had persuaded them both that Rose promised to raise their children in the church.

Douglas had been making good money as a beginning engineer at Todd and Company and Rose and he seemed happy and bought a FHA home. Richard came along shortly after Melinda turned two. Because of his ROTC commitment Douglas had had to go to serve in Vietnam. At first, Dolores thought that Rose would go home to Tennessee to her family, but her parents were so angry that she hadn't finished college that they said they didn't want her or the "brats." Dolores knew that this had hurt Rose's feelings, and wondered if that was one of the reasons she was searching for acceptance from other men now. At least Rose was bringing the children here before inviting men into her house.

Frequently Dolores was tempted to talk over her problems with Father Flynn. He was new to the parish and didn't know any of the parishioners well. If it had been old Father Duffy it would have been a lot easier. Something had to be done but it was hard talking about such a personal problem to a stranger. Maybe when she went to mass tomorrow morning she would stay after and talk to the Father. She knew that she wouldn't make mass today. She dearly would have liked to go but the children had no extra clothing. She had sent them home on Wednesday with the last of the extra clothing she had managed to get cheap at the thrift store. They were still wearing the clothes and they were filthy.

"Stop bothering me, I'm still sleepy!" Melinda cried. Dolores had been so lost in thought that she hadn't noticed Richard had scooted off his chair and was now shaking Melinda. He climbed up on the couch and put his arms around his sister and hugged her hard.

"Leave Melinda alone, Richard," Dolores said. "Come on upstairs with me and I'll dunk you in the tub. It's so hot I have a good mind to put you in clothes and all. You must have sat down in that crud in the alley. Your pants are black!"

As Richard reluctantly followed his grandmother up the steps, Melinda rubbed her head. It hurt and there was a big lump on the back that she must have gotten when she fell off the chair. She tried to remember what had happened. The last thing she recalled was putting her head down on the table then feeling herself slipping down, down, down into a dark tunnel. Her head often hurt when she got up. and she knew there wasn't any use complaining to Rose so she was learning to live with it.

An empty stomach reminded her of the milk she had been waiting for when she fell. Melinda walked over to the kitchen and helped herself to a bowl of the Superchex and poured herself a large glass of milk. Loud protests were coming from upstairs. Richard hated getting his head washed. Melinda knew Grandma was scrubbing to get his blond curls back to their light color. She put all the food away and marched up the steps for she knew that she would be next.

"Stop yelling" Dolores said to the screaming boy. "If you'd stay still I could rinse this soap off your head and not get it in your eyes. Seems like this 'No more Tears stuff' doesn't work any better than plain old shampoo."

Melinda stood quietly in the doorway, watching her Grandma struggle with the squirming youngster. Finally she went over and held Richard's hands so that it was easier to rinse the soap from his head. Rivulets of gray ran down his back as the water was poured over and over through his blond hair. Richard must have put his head down in the alley when he had slipped from Melinda's grasp. After a few minutes the rinsing was through and Richard calmed down.

"I really should give it another soaping but this child, is almost impossible," Dolores complained. "Out you go. Wrap yourself up in this big towel; it's your father's favorite. You can go around naked for a while until your pants dry."

The water was draining out of the tub, leaving a soapy

scum behind on the edge as it trickled down the pipes. "I'll scrub the tub before you get in, don't worry, Melinda," Dolores winked at her. "That boy sure was dirty. Haven't had such a dirty mess since your dad slipped in the mud while he was trying to sled on a melting snowy hill."

"I can take care of myself, I can even wash my own head," Melinda smiled. She didn't want her grandma to feel the bump at the back because she knew that it might mean a trip to the clinic. She hated the clinic even worse than going down the dark alley. You always had to wait and wait and wait and then when the doctor did look at you he didn't pay attention to what you told him. Sometimes it almost seemed that because you were a child you didn't even exist. He didn't pay much more attention to her mother or grandma either but since it was always a different doctor anyway, Melinda decided that it was kind of like television. You were on one side of the TV and no matter how you felt, the TV was going to go right on talking and solving problems whether you had them or not.

Since Richard was already rooting in the closet in Douglas' room trying to find something to play with, Dolores left Melinda to bathe herself. She was always amazed at how bright this four-year-old was and how adept at handling her brother. It reminded Dolores of when Doug was small. He'd been reading when he was only three and a half and it seemed his daughter took after him. Maybe it was just as well since Rose wasn't giving either of the children much of her time and attention these days.

After lunch, both children took long naps and Dolores stretched out on the couch to catch up on the rest she'd lost the night before. The children had been good. Richard was active, building with the odds and ends left over from the block set that Doug had used when he was a kid. Melinda loved looking at the picture books and coloring.

About two-thirty Tilly, Dolores' sister, stopped by to see if everything was all right, since she had missed Dolores at mass. Both the children were still sleeping but Tilly could tell that they were there from the toys strewn around the room.

"Got stuck baby-sitting again, did you?" Tilly's voice took on a mocking tone. Tilly's grandchildren lived in Nova Scotia and it was only for two weeks each summer that she got to see them.

"Well at least I get to see Doug's children often. I don't mind." Dolores held her tongue, not wanting to share the whole story with her sister, who tended to be the kind that would say, "I told you so." Tilly had agreed with Allen's concern that Rose wasn't a Catholic. She also pretended not to understand Rose's Southern accent.

"Harry and I are going up to the lake tomorrow. Want to come along? I thought we'd pack a picnic and spend the day under the trees while he fished."

"Sure, it will be good to get away from this heat. Those buildings cut off the nice breezes I used to get and I've not been to the lake since Allen died." Dolores jumped at the chance for a drive with her brother-in-law and Till in the country.

Their conversation must have awakened Richard, for he began to whimper. Dolores went up the steps and picked him up. He was dripping with perspiration and cranky like he always was when he first woke up. As she was carrying him down the stairs Dolores could see no motion from her open bedroom. Melinda must still be sleeping.

"Isn't he getting to look a lot like Doug? All these blond ringlets," Dolores ran her fingers through the awakening boy's hair. He cuddled up on her lap and soon stopped complaining as he listened for a while to their casual chit chat.

In a few moments he slipped down to the floor and

crawled over to the blocks in the corner and began to stack them in rows and run a toy car between them. The two women went on talking about some of the old friends that they might see while they were picnicking the following day. There was a hotel at the lake that was popular with quite a few of the Dimsdale residents. In fact, one summer Dolores and Allen had spent a week there on their vacation.

Tilly looked at her watch. "My goodness! It's past three and I have to put a roast in the oven for dinner. Too bad you can't come home with me. That's one of the reasons I stopped. When is Rose coming home to pick up the kids? I could come back for you around six then you could stay over and we could get an early start tomorrow."

"Some other time," Dolores smiled.

It would have been easy for Tilly to have taken them all over to her house in her Chevy, but Dolores knew Till didn't want to invite the children. She didn't answer the question, since she never knew when Rose might show up.

After Tilly left, Dolores called upstairs to wake Melinda. When there was no reply, Dolores climbed the steps again. Melinda was sound asleep, clutching her doll in her arms. For a little while Dolores stared at the pale thin child then, placing her hand on Melinda's shoulder, she called her again. This time the little girl's eyes opened slowly and she stared at her grandmother almost as though she couldn't remember who or where she was.

"Come on downstairs, love," Dolores said. "It is much cooler and I need you to help me while I get the stew ready for supper." This was an invitation that always pleased Melinda, and she gave her grandma a small smile and put her foot over the side of the bed. Her head was still hurting and she seemed to be having a hard time waking up.

"I'll be down in a few minutes. I think I have to get some water on my face first. Your bed was comfortable. I slept extra long, didn't I? What time is it? Did I miss the cartoons?"

"Why goodness, child, that program was over hours ago. You were a sleepyhead but last night none of us got much sleep. Richard is downstairs playing. Come down when you are awake." Dolores ran her hand over Melinda's head. "That's a nasty bump you have on the back of your head. Must have happened when you fell last night. I'll get some ice and when you come down we'll see if that will help it go down. I don't like it that you've been sleeping so long, too. I'll tell your mama that she should take you to the clinic. It's too late today. We'd never get home with the short staff on Sunday."

Dolores was wondering when Rose would come to pick up the children. She usually came sailing in after one in the afternoon from one of her late-night dates. She would probably show up for dinner, since she never refused a free meal. Melinda sat still on the couch while her grandma placed a bag of ice on her head. It hurt when the ice touched the bump but she was too groggy to protest.

As though she could tell what her grandma was thinking, Melinda remarked, "Ma said she might not be home until Monday if she was lucky, whatever that means. Can't I help with the carrots while I hold the ice on with one hand?"

Dolores busied herself in the kitchen and motioned for Melinda to join her. "Just sit at the table and cut the vegetables after I peel them. That will be a big help."

She wasn't prepared to have the children stay another night. That would mean that she would probably miss the trip with Till and have to face the sarcastic remarks that would bring. After she got the stew going she thought about the excuses she might give for not going rather than have Till show up and see that she still had the children.

As she opened the refrigerator, she noticed that she was

12

running out of milk and it was too far to drag the children to the store. They would have to manage with what they had in the house. Keeping the children frequently dug into any extra savings she had, but she never begrudged the money that it took. She was sure that Douglas, when he came home, would make it up to her. It wasn't until long past supper and putting the children to bed that the phone rang. The operator said it was a collect call. Dolores, hoping that it was Rose, accepted it.

Every time there was a collect call she was afraid it might be about Doug.

"Hi, Mom," Rose's voice sounded husky, "bet you can't guess where I am. I'm in Atlantic City having fun, fun, fun." Her voice trailed off. *She's probably drunk*, Dolores thought.

"When are you coming home? I've been invited to the lake tomorrow and if you get here early I could still go."

"Sounds like fun," the slurred voice mingled with the rock music in the background. "Tommy, when ya gonna take me home?"

Dolores waited while she listened to some mumbled conversation to the beat of conga drums. The line went dead. After waiting for fifteen minutes it became obvious that there wouldn't be any answer until Rose and Tommy, or whoever it was, sobered up. It would take at least six hours to drive from Atlantic City to Dimsdale. Even though it was late Dolores called Till with the lame excuse that she had a stomach bug and she wouldn't be able to go with them the following day.

"Got stuck with them again, did you?" Till saw through the ploy immediately. Was this the time to spill the beans? Dolores bit her tongue and forced back the tears. She wasn't going to let Till know how frustrated and disappointed she was.

13

"I'll call you when I feel better," she replied and said her good-byes quickly before Till had a chance to force her to admit that the children were still there.

2

Douglas

Chaplain Greig stopped scribbling on the discharge papers and glanced at the dejected captain sitting, head bowed, across the desk. Douglas' thoughts whirled round and round. Only yesterday he had been laying out a new road far to the north. It seemed impossible that he was being sent home. The reason had seemed so vague that he hesitated to ask the chaplain to repeat the paragraph he had read about his mother, his wife, and his children. None of it made any sense. Until now all the news from home had been sporadic but with no hint of problems.

"You say that I'm being discharged to take care of pressing family matters? Doesn't that telegram explain why my family needs me? Maybe it says something about someone being deathly ill and you don't want to tell me. I've been here for quite a while and seen all kinds of sickness and death. I can take it. I want to serve out my time unless it is something horrible."

Looking down at the yellow sheet in front of him, Bill Greig frowned. He'd read it twice and knew that the Red Cross didn't ask for this kind of discharge unless there was an emergency. It was hard to judge, but someone in Washington had been given more information than they cared to share with either Douglas or himself. The information would probably come long after Douglas had gone.

"I guess you'll have to wait until you get home to find

out. There will be a plane leaving at nine hundred hours tomorrow. Get your gear together and be ready to go along. You might look up the people at the Red Cross in Dimsdale when you get back. The request came through them."

Bill stood and extended his hand to Doug, signifying the interview was ended. "Thank you, I guess," Doug said, stretching his six-foot-three frame to a military salute. "Under other circumstances I suppose I should be glad to be getting out, but since I don't know why, I feel scared. Even more scared than when I was dodging bullets."

Strolling out into the humid evening, Douglas glanced at the busy army base. It hardly seemed possible that in just a few hours he would be leaving and on a plane headed home. It would probably be two days until he got home, but everything was happening too fast. Thinking Army engineering for months was hard to shake.

He noted that one of the trucks carrying a load of wood was improperly stacked. Through force of habit he stopped the driver to order him to redo the load. Not until he walked on did it dawn on him that he no longer had the authority to tell any of these G.I.s what to do. As he passed by the PX Doug decided that he'd better spend what was left of his money on a few gifts to take home. There were many items for sale that would do for his mother and wife but for the kids he shook his head. The Army in the field didn't think of amusing toys or even children's-sized clothing. Perfume, kimonos, and pretty fans were there for enticing local entertainment. The Army was funny that way. It didn't want you to fraternize but made it easy to do it.

At chow, he hardly spoke to the other officers. They were asking all kinds of questions about the progress in the north and he felt embarrassed to admit he wasn't returning there, so he shared the news of his discharge with no one. It was hard getting to sleep. Most nights in the field he had only to imagine his arms around Rose and the softness of her body to make him drift off. Since he would soon be able to touch her and hold her for real, the image wouldn't suffice. The excitement of seeing the children finally began to register. He'd missed them more than he'd realized. It wasn't until the possibility of actually seeing them that his desire, long sublimated, surfaced.

Richard had been only fifteen months when Doug had left home. From the few pictures he'd gotten he knew he was much bigger. He began to worry that Richard might not remember him. It would be good to see Ma, too, and try to get her out of that miserable shack. He finally fell asleep making plans for a house on the outskirts of town with a small apartment on the second floor for Ma.

When the plane took off promptly in the morning, most of his worry about why he was being summoned home so unexpectantly had been dispelled by the anticipation of seeing his family. It had also dawned on him that in a few weeks he would be back at his desk at his job, where he'd be making decisions on civilian engineering that would be permanent, not temporary like all the construction he'd been planning for the past few months.

The plane was a cargo plane which was returning empty except for a few wooden crates. Only he and three other G.I.s were in the huge fuselage. They were carrying large duffel bags and either sat or lay on them since there were no seats. Although he longed to talk to them about his discharge, he hesitated, since they probably wouldn't understand why and he couldn't explain either. They had served their tour of duty and had every right for their joking behavior. He listened as they talked about their favorite beer joints, food, girls, family and the entertainment that was only hours away.

Near dinner time they circled the air field in Hawaii. When they landed, Doug was surprised when a captain approached him as he got off the plane.

"Captain Dixon?" the shorter older man inquired. "I've been asked to take care of you and see that you get on a commercial plane to Frisco. This plane will refuel, reload and go back."

"What about the other men?" asked Doug.

The captain smiled. "They will wait here at the base until a military plane can take them on to the States. The chaplain felt your trip should be expedited and we've arranged to have you go by TWA. We'll have to hurry though, your flight takes off in about an hour. I have a taxi waiting at the gate. Can you manage your bag?"

Doug frowned. He didn't like this kind of special treatment. Even though he was an officer, he felt the other enlisted men deserved a chance to be able to go home as quickly. But he knew there was no arguing with the system. He picked up his bag and hurried after the swiftly departing captain.

The captain, who identified himself as Tim Gray, talked over his shoulder the long walk to the gate, telling Doug how sorry he was that he was stuck at a desk job here instead of being at the "front." Doug didn't reply. Captain Gray hustled Doug through the gate and opened the door to the cab and almost pushed Doug inside. To the driver he said, "Airport and hurry!"

Before he had a chance to say thank you, Doug found an envelope with an airplane ticket put into his extended hand and the door shut in his face. The cab driver pulled out and at breakneck speed scurried in and out of traffic and across town. This was the first Doug had seen of a city not in the war zone in eleven months. It seemed peculiar to see so much color and people moving at what looked like a snail's pace.

It was almost as if the war didn't exist. This seemed way out of pace with what he had just left. Since he'd never seen anything of Hawaii on the way to Vietnam, he gawked. The diverse population and informal dress seemed strange but pleasant. He wished he could spend some time here and not be hurried off on the next flight. He was so busy watching all that was going on outside the tab that he was surprised when the scenery changed abruptly and he knew that in a few minutes he would be inside the large air terminal.

As he left the cab, he attempted to pay the cab driver. "No, sir, your ride was paid before we left. I hope you have a safe trip home. I am always glad to send someone in the other direction. My brother is over there where you just left and my father will be glad to see him come home for good in four months. This is a crazy war, if you ask me." Doug fished in his pocket and offered a crumpled bill.

The driver pushed it back in his hand. "Save it for a beer on me when you get back. Just head in those doors and you see the TWA gates on your left."

The boarding sign was up on Gate three and the loudspeaker announced that the flight for Frisco was leaving in twelve minutes. Doug went through the monitoring station at full stride and extended his ticket to the uniformed girl who was guiding passengers onto the ramp to board.

"Glad to have you traveling with us, Captain," the girl said, and smiled. It was incredible to see a female this close. She joined with the obviously relaxed returning vacationers in searching out his seat. Getting used to being a civilian would be harder than Doug had anticipated. He swung his bag overhead and settled for the center seat between a girl with a lei and an elderly man with a blue-printed Hawaiian shirt.

Even being served dinner on the tray after they were airborne was an unexpectedly delicious experience. He particularly enjoyed the fresh pineapple. The girl next to the window kept trying to ask him about the war and wanted to give him a day-by-day description of her stay on the island. After a while when she realized Doug was not responding she reached in her bag for a paperback book.

Sleep was fast coming. The trip and change of time zones made it hard to keep his eyes open. Doug slept until the plane's pilot announced that seat belts should be buckled, that they would be arriving in San Francisco shortly.

When Doug got off the plane, he stretched and made for a rest room. He needed a shave and to freshen up. He decided that since his flight for LaGuardia was six hours away he might try to see some of the town even at this early hour in the morning.

*   *   *

The houses on Pearl Street seemed a lot smaller than Douglas had remembered. He drove slowly down the three-hundred block in a car he had rented, searching for his old Buick, which had always been parked in the drive in front of 316. The lawn was newly mowed and marigolds and petunias were blooming profusely in the beds in front of the house. Doug was amazed at how pretty the house looked, and how Rose had taken care of the garden. He was puzzled that his Buick wasn't where he expected. Perhaps Rose had learned to drive and was out with the kids. After all, she probably didn't know he was coming back and might be shopping.

Excitedly, he hopped out of the Ford and ran up the walk and tried the door. It swung open and Doug was surprised to see all new furniture, drapes and rugs in the front room.

"Rose, I'm home!" he sang out. A strange woman with a scarf tied around her head came bustling out of the kitchen. When she saw Doug she let out a yell and took the broom she was carrying and placed it across the front of her as if in self-defense. "Who are you? What do you mean barging into our house like this?" she asked.

"Sorry!" Douglas backed up a few steps. His thoughts

were in total confusion. "When I left eleven months ago we were renting this house and I didn't know that my wife and kids had moved out. Do you know where they are? I've been sent home because of some family emergency. How long ago did she move out of here?"

Relaxing her hold on the broom, Matilda Farnsworth beckoned Doug toward the couch.

"You sure ask a lot of questions, Captain. I can't tell you much. Only what I've heard from the neighbors. We moved in here just before Christmas. She wasn't living here then. The place was a mess and some of the furniture was still here. It was all such a wreck that we junked it. Seems like she took some of the furniture and moved out, in October. No one around here knows where she went. She'd been having some wild parties before she left and none of the neighbors wanted to keep in touch. They do say that you have cute kids. Can't give you any more information. Want a drink? You look bushed."

Wild parties? Nine months ago? What had happened to Rose and his children? Douglas shook his head in disbelief. All his imagined homecoming ideas were gone. He was shaken to the core. Politely he refused the offered drink, thanked Matilda for the information, and walked slowly back to the car. The only thing he could think of was that she must have moved in with Ma and didn't want to worry him since he had still been sending his mail to 316 Pearl and she'd never given him any hint in her letters to let him know that she had moved. *Had she used up all their savings and been forced to get out of the house?* He sat for quite a while before starting the car. *What had happened to his car?* He certainly did have a lot of questions.

Making a U-turn he headed back to the center of Dimsdale. It was still early in the morning and it pleased him to see the children riding their bikes and playing in the yards as he

21

passed through the suburbs. Starting in the business district he noticed traffic heavier than he remembered just a few months before. The war had brought some new people to town along with the expanding plant defense contracts. Dimsdale wasn't a sleepy upstate town anymore.

It was hard to find a parking space on Queen Street near the alley to Ma's, so he turned the corner and parked on Tenth. Walking back, he noticed that already the bars were doing a brisk business. He hurried past a few lolling half-drunken men and turned into the alley, which hadn't been cleaned in years, if ever.

"What a dump of a place for Ma to live." He told himself again that as soon as possible he'd make sure she could move into better surroundings. His steps quickened as he saw the porch and open screen door to the small house. Taking the steps two at a time, Doug shouted, "Hello!" as he burst into the tiny living room. Melinda, who was playing with her doll, looked up and, slowly comprehending, gave a wild leap into his arms.

The two of them stood clutching one another tightly, tears running down both their faces.

"Daddy, Daddy, I'm so glad to see you! It's been so long. I missed you so much. Are you going to stay home now? I never want you to go away." The words kept spilling out of the small child as she clung to her father.

Douglas was speechless. His glance went around the room searching for Richard, Rose, his mother. Finally Aunt Tilly came down the steps. "What are you doing here, Aunt Till? Where is everyone? Is Ma home? Why was I sent for? What's the matter?"

"Sit down, Douglas. I'll tell you all about it. Richard is taking an early nap upstairs and your ma is recovering from a bout of summer pneumonia. I came over a week ago, and she was hardly able to walk around. I've been holding down the fort ever since. The doctor says she'll be fine in a week or so. She just needs rest right now. He arranged with the Red Cross for you to be sent home to help take care of things. I'm so glad you came so quickly. I would have met you at the airport in Albany, but I've not been out of the house, what with taking care of your ma and the children." Till sat back. Her lined face showing the wear and tear of the past week. It was Doug's turn to take over.

"What about Rose? Hasn't she been helping?" Doug frowned at the news. Of course he was worried about his mother, but still, he didn't see why her illness was enough for him to have been given a discharge. Something was missing.

"We don't know where Rose is," Till replied.

"What do you mean? Has something happened to her?" Doug went over and put both his hands on his aunt's shoulders and looked her straight in the eyes.

"Douglas, I'm telling you the truth. We really don't know where she is, let alone if she is all right. She called your ma late one night five weeks ago and said she was in Atlantic City. When she didn't come home after a week your ma asked the police to check it out and they can't find a thing. That's why we think you'll have to take over caring for these children. It's just too much for your ma. Otherwise they will put them in foster care. You know how your ma fussed when she heard that. She made the doctor promise to ask for them to send you home. That's the whole story."

Melinda tugged on Doug's pant leg. "You'll take care of us, won't you, Daddy? Richard misses Mamma so much. He's been crying a lot. Granny took good care of us, but now she's sick."

As Douglas again lifted the four-year-old into his arms he turned from his own problems to comfort his daughter. The tears were streaming down her cheeks, although she wasn't sobbing aloud. *What was the matter with Rose to disappear like this? Something must have happened to her or she surely would have gotten back to care for the children.*

"What was she doing in Atlantic City?"

"I guess you'll find out sooner or later." Till smirked. Secretly she was pleased to tell Doug about Rose. Till hadn't thought Rose was a good match for Doug to begin with. "Rose had been dating a lot of fellows since you left. The night she left for Atlantic City the children say she was with a sailor. His name was Tom. She told your ma that the following night when she called from Atlantic City. That's the last we heard from her. Your ma says she sounded drunk.

"She never seemed the home body type to me." Till began to let out all her ire and frustration at being stuck taking care of both the children and her sister this past week. "You know your father and I always told you that marrying out of the faith was wrong. See what a mess you've gotten us all into. These poor tykes have been left with your ma time and time again, while she was lally-gagging around. She's used up all the money she got from selling your car and furniture on snappy clothing for herself. It'll be best if she does get lost and doesn't come home. Good riddance, if you ask me."

"Please, not in front of Melinda," Douglas interrupted the flow of rhetoric. He had heard his aunt's tirades before and wanted to spare not only Melinda but himself any more. It was hard enough to digest the information that his wife was missing, without all the additional details. It didn't seem like the Rose he'd left behind. He began to wonder just how well he knew Rose. Their whirlwind romance hadn't given time for great introspective discourse. Maybe having the babies so close together had made her unhappy. Maybe she was still too young to be saddled with the responsibility of taking care of everything alone.

"I'm going upstairs to see Ma." Doug went to the stairs still carrying Melinda. Her small arms wound so tightly around his neck spoke eloquently of her need for protection and comfort. He took a handkerchief from his pocket and dabbed her eyes. "Don't worry, darling, Daddy's going to take care of everything. He isn't going to have to go back and be away from you again. I promise."

He felt the grip loosen slightly but he kept holding the child as he climbed the steps. Ma's room seemed extremely hot, despite the small fan propped up on the only chair next to her bed. The room was so small that even though the double bed was pushed next to the wall there was scarcely enough room to walk between the dresser and the bed on the other side. Dolores seemed to be asleep, and Douglas stood for several minutes looking at her thin frame outlined under the damp sheet. Before he could speak she opened her eyes and smiled brightly.

"I knew you'd come as soon as you could. It is so good to see you. I'm so sorry to bother you like this. Till and the doctor said it was the only thing we could do. Did Till tell you about Rose? Don't worry about me. I'll be fine. Give your old ma a big hug. I'm not contagious."

Doug put Melinda down and bent over and hugged his mother gently. Even with her gray hair spread out on the pillow she didn't look much older than sixty. Her face still had few lines and her eyes were deep set and alert, giving her face a knowing expression. He patted her leg, and although he had many questions about Rose to ask, he was content to wait until she was up and around to ask them. Besides which, he didn't want Melinda to hear any more details that might be unkind about her mother.

Dolores closed her eyes and smiled. Even though she had fought with the doctor and Till about getting Doug released from the Army, she felt glad he was here and could take over the responsibility. She could feel the tension in her body start to relax. Starting at her toes and going on up through the muscles of her body, the weight of the worry slipped off. Soon she was in a sound sleep. No longer was the dream of houses full of children demanding attention. She was dreaming of picnicking at the lake with Allen when they were both young.

By the time Doug came down the steps Tilly had her carry-all bag in her hand all packed and ready to go. She stood next to the door and said her farewells together with a long list of the do's and don'ts about the children and Dolores's care. Once they were alone, Douglas and Melinda sat together on the couch. Melinda had lots of questions about the war and told about moving out of the house and into the efficiency room and in an innocent way described how Rose had kept going out to make money with some nice men and how proud she was to have taken good care of Richard.

"Mama must have missed you almost as much as I did," Melinda said. "Whenever she would get one of your letters she would cry and cry. Sometimes then she would get mad at Richard and me. I think she was sad that you weren't here. Sometimes she'd say things like, 'Boy if your Dad was here I'd really blow this joint.' I know she missed you."

A soft cry came from upstairs. It quickly escalated into a howl. Douglas jumped up. For a moment he was bewildered, then he remembered his son who had apparently just awakened.

Both Doug and Melinda rushed up the stairs. "Richard is always like this when he wakes up from his nap. I'll pat his back for a while and he'll calm down," Melinda explained.

The awakening child stared at the tall man in uniform who had entered his room and stood smiling over the crib. His sobbing ebbed while Melinda stroked his back, but when Doug bent over and started to pick him up, Richard shied away and reached his arms up to his sister.

"This is our Dad, Richard. You know the one in the pictures in Granny's picture book. He's come home to take care of us because they don't know where Mamma is."

It was obvious that she understood a lot more about what had been going on than Douglas would have cared for her to know. Reaching over again to pick his son up, he was pleased that the child allowed him to with no further complaint. The boy was very heavy, almost heavier than Melinda. As they proceeded down the steps, Richard's curiosity about the pins and buttons on the uniform kept him occupied. By the time they were again all seated on the couch, this time with Richard on Doug's lap, the child was able to give a small smile in response to Doug's remarks about how much being away from the family had been hard on them all.

The following days went by swiftly. Every day Doug got better and better acquainted with his children and their daily routines. By the following Friday, he was able to help Dolores come down and sit in the living room for an hour. The doctor said she was improving nicely and could be up for a while each day.

Dolores, too, was enjoying the attention and presence of her son and felt comfortable being left alone once in awhile so Doug could do the shopping and take care of errands. Douglas was arranging over the phone to go back to his old job and had a realtor looking for a place to rent.

One thing Dolores didn't protest. Douglas insisted that she move in to the new house with them. Her furniture wasn't much but it would save them having to buy all new. Doug had discovered soon after he'd arrived that the savings account that he had when he left had been closed. The place Rose had rented had taken what furniture there was and sold it when she hadn't returned in exchange for back rent. It would be a few months until Doug would be able to get his financial feet on the ground. The realtor doubted anyone would attempt to buy Dolores's house even to make an additional parking space now that all the buildings surrounded it.

3

Esmirelda

"How lucky I am," Esmirelda Garcia said aloud as she pinned the large white gardenia in her hair. Never in her wildest dreams would she have imagined that this was happening. She patted her slightly protruding stomach and again said aloud. "You get all the credit for this."

In only an hour she would be standing in the Dixon's living room saying her vows to Doug. When he had moved next door in September, she had peeked through the blinds as he helped carry the few furnishings from the U-Haul. She had seen the two children scampering around on the lawn and the elderly woman who came to the porch occasionally to call to them. Getting to know them had been easy. Esmirelda's daughter, Charmain, was the same age as Melinda. When Doug found that Esmirelda's husband had been killed in an industrial accident, conversation became easy. They somehow had a mutual grief.

Esmirelda had sympathized with his vain search for his wife. Even though she was several years older than Doug and no longer slim, she began to hope she might romantically interest him. One evening when the children were asleep and he'd visited, she had managed to seduce him. She had been without any sexual activity for over a year and they had a long intense lovemaking session. When he returned night after night, she had begun to hope that he would eventually think of her as a prospective bride. All of the lovemaking was rough. It seemed as though Doug was punishing her for what Rose had done to him.

Except for the first few nights, Doug had always worn a condom, and since it had been such a long time since Esmirelda had had to worry about birth control, it came as a surprise when she had missed her period. The doctor confirmed in a few weeks that indeed she was pregnant. Douglas hadn't taken the news well. He'd been happy that he had been having fun at the house next door. He wasn't ready for a commitment. Besides he wasn't free to think about marriage until he knew what had happened to Rose. The police in Atlantic City thought she was a victim of foul play. Until either she or her body showed up, Doug wasn't able to legally marry again. Since both Esmirelda and Doug were Catholic, he knew Esmirelda would never consider an abortion.

Douglas wasn't in love with Esmirelda. She had some good traits and seemed to love both Richard and Melinda. He began to blame Es for trapping him into a corner. For a few weeks he'd stopped going over to her house completely. Soon it became extremely obvious that Esmirelda was going to make it difficult. Even though the days were getting colder she would come out to rake the leaves in shorts and a halter. Watching her bending over, partially exposing her ample breasts, was torture. The memory of caressing her rotund body haunted him at night. Her extra desserts that arrived daily were a constant reminder that she was trying to please not only Doug but his mother and children.

Just by chance she was in the kitchen talking to Dolores when the phone rang the day before Ash Wednesday. Dolores called Doug. He couldn't avoid talking with Esmirelda there. The call was from the New Jersey State Police. They had found the remains of a body in the woods outside of Trenton. They had identified it as Rose after checking dental records. She had been murdered. They asked what arrangements he

29

was going to make to take care of what was left of the body. It had been in the woods about two weeks and had badly decomposed.

It must have been from the conversation and his expression that Esmirelda concluded that the obstacle that had been in her way was magically removed. She came over and put her arms around Doug. "You must be relieved to hear that you won't have to worry anymore. I'm sorry that she had to die like that. Come over after dinner and we can talk. I want to show you Charmain's confirmation dress like the one I made for Melinda. They'll look like twins."

Doug gently got out of her embrace. He was embarrassed that she was so forward in front of Dolores and that she had immediately jumped to the conclusion that everything was now on for them. The news had upset him. During the past two months he had gradually acknowledged that Rose wasn't going to return. He'd been busy getting used to his newly expanded job and responsibilities at home. He didn't know how to handle the invitation from Es. Since Dolores was staring at them both and since she had never observed any show of affection between them before, she didn't know what was happening.

"I'll come over for a little while. I've brought home a lot of paperwork, and I'll have to arrange for Rose's funeral. I will also have to call her family in Tennessee. Maybe they would want to have her buried there. It would be better like that. I'd like to spare the kids having to go. It will be bad enough telling them that their mother is dead. They've just about gotten used to the fact that she isn't here."

After Esmirelda left, Dolores bluntly asked, "What's going on with you two?" Indicating with her head the departing neighbor. "I knew you'd been going over there at night for a while, but I didn't know any hanky panky was happening. She has been asking a lot about you lately. I thought you'd stopped going over and she wanted to find out from me if you were angry."

"You might as well know. Es is pregnant. I'm sure now that she knows Rose is dead she will want me to marry her. What do you think? I'm not in love with her, but I know she's fond of the children and Melinda would have Charmain as a half-sister. That kid is here most of the time as it is. They might as well be sisters."

Dolores sat down heavily on the nearest kitchen chair. She sat thinking for a long time before she answered Doug. There were many things she liked about Es. She had become dependent on her for shopping and for company during the afternoons when the girls were in kindergarten and Richard was napping.

"You're the one who has to make the decision," she finally replied. "You know I like Esmirelda and Charmain very much. It all depends on a lot of things. There are plenty of reasons you should but I guess the most pressing one is the fact she is pregnant. How many months along?"

"Going on five I think." Doug hung his head. "I'm going in the other room to make some phone calls. It's Saturday. I hope some of Rose's family are home, and that they'll not blame me for the fact she is dead. Her dad is mighty mad that I told him she was missing. That's a strange family. They've blamed me for everything since the wedding. Who do I call for an undertaker? I hope all this won't cost too much. I've just about gotten enough in the bank that I can plan on buying a house soon."

It took a long time to arrange the details of the funeral. Fortunately Rose's mother was the one who answered the phone. She took the news with a resignation Doug found hard to believe. Without consulting other members of the family immediately, Rose's mother told him to arrange for the body to be sent to Hallowmens Glen. There was only one undertaker in Rose's small town so there wasn't even a question about that. When Doug suggested he come down for the funeral, Mrs. Slocum was direct.

"Don't bother yourself," she replied. "Hirum will have a tough time as it is. I'm afraid he might git out his shotgun. Neber did git ober ya stealin' Rose."

Douglas put down the phone and sat with his head on the desk. There were lots of unanswered questions. Where had Rose been these past months? Even though Doug had gotten used to the idea that she was never returning, there was always that slender hope in the back of his mind that she might. In a way, however, his love for her had disappeared gradually until there was only a ghost of memories that looking at the children brought.

He'd hoped that he could go to the funeral. It somehow would have meant that in saying farewell he'd be able to bury the past as well. Strangely, he didn't hate Rose, but couldn't understand why she had run away and needed other men. As for her family, he'd never expected them to be happy with him. But he was disappointed that they didn't even acknowledge the grandchildren. Except for pictures, they hadn't seen the children. Even at Christmas and their birthdays, they sent no presents for Richard and Melinda.

Making arrangements with McMurtry's Funeral Home had been simple since there was to be no open casket. Although Doug should have felt relieved after his last phone call, he still felt as though the second shoe hadn't dropped. He roamed the house knowing that until he told the children the bitterness wouldn't leave his mouth.

Richard, Charmain, and Melinda had been playing hide-and-seek in the bedrooms. The ruckus was happy as they ran back and forth overhead. He'd wait until after dinner. He still had plenty of decisions to make. His thoughts turned to the dilemma next door. He had to make a move, one way or another. It seemed easier to ignore Esmirelda's pregnancy when he couldn't marry her. Although he'd told her he'd support the child. That was as much as he'd ever promised until now.

Since Doug wanted to sort out his feelings, he finally decided to confront Esmirelda during the day, and not wait until evening. Shouting to Dolores that he was going over to Es's he hurried out the front door.

No one was on the first floor as he entered the house. He called upstairs and waited for a reply. When there was none, Doug thought Es might be sewing in the back bedroom, and couldn't hear him. After waiting impatiently for a few more minutes, Doug climbed the steps. By now he had strengthened his desire to settle the problems once and for all. When he got to the landing he heard water running from the back bedroom bath. Suddenly it stopped and before he could say anything Esmirelda came into the hall. She was drying herself with a bath towel. Her hair was dripping wet and even though they had made love many times he had never seen her naked.

Her pendulous breasts had developed large brown rings around the protruding nipples. They seemed much larger than he remembered. Her abdomen, now fully revealed, had a slight fullness over the navel. Doug remembered how delighted he'd been when he'd reached over the first time and felt Melinda stirring within Rose. The urge to reach over and feel the movement of this unborn child made him step closer.

Esmirelda took this as a signal to lower the towel. The tears started rolling down her cheeks. As she closed the distance between them in a few strides she didn't take her eyes from Douglas. Although she was crying, a radiant smile came over her face

"I knew you'd come over sooner or later. I wanted to get dressed 'specially for you."

33

She leaned against Doug's chest. Her head just reached his chin and he buried his face in her fragrant wet hair. Automatically his hands reached up to hold both of her breasts. He slid them next to her stomach and over her still wet thighs. Without thinking, he picked her up and carried her into the front bedroom.

Quickly shedding his clothing he joined her on the bed. For the first time in many months he found himself making love to Es. Somehow this time it was different. No longer was Rose in the back of his mind as he caressed and fondled all of Es's body. He was not in a hurry. Gradually he realized he was enjoying the lovemaking in a new way.

As they both lay quiet after their climax, Doug reached over and put his hand on her belly. "Do you mind if I wait to see if I can feel the baby move?"

"He's quite active. You won't have long to wait, unless he's as contented as I am right now. I want a nap. Stay here and rest with me for a while."

In a few moments the baby moved against Douglas' hand. He felt fulfilled. He got out of bed and slowly donned his shirt and pants as he watched Es drift off to sleep. Without speaking about it, he realized that both of them had made a decision. In a few weeks they'd be married. Already the families had started to integrate. Maybe this would work out just fine.

4

Dolores

What went wrong? When did it start? Six months had gone by since Doug had married Esmirelda. The baby boy named Sam had arrived and seemed to be giving both Doug and Es a mutual interest that bridged their earlier marriage distancing. Now Charmain and Melinda were sharing the back bedroom and appeared to be best friends. Richard welcomed the new baby, glad for a boy to balance the mostly female household.

Dolores wondered if maybe she'd seen it coming even before the baby came. Es wanted to do all the cooking after a few weeks. They had decided that since she owned her house they would all move into her home. The houses were the same and it was only natural that Es felt at home in her own kitchen. She also liked to cook with more spices than any of them were accustomed to having in their food. Dolores felt perfectly content to prepare vegetables and do the clean up and most of the cleaning and ironing.

Once the baby arrived it meant that since Dolores was sleeping with Richard and the house had only three bedrooms, the baby would be placed in her room, too. During the night Es would come in to nurse the baby, but Dolores didn't complain.

In August, tension between the two women was beginning to be obvious. One afternoon Melinda had come in from swimming and collapsed on the kitchen floor. Es became angry when Dolores picked Melinda up and carried her in to the couch.

"She's demanding attention again. I'm tired of her laying down and twitching like that when she can't get her way. She must have had a fuss with Charmain. Last week it happened up in their room. Charmain said it had happened several times before and she always stopped after a while. Get her off the couch. She's all wet!" Es stormed. She grabbed Melinda and shook her.

"Stop fooling around, kiddo, and open your eyes and look at me. I'm not standing for any more of this behavior."

Melinda remained limp and Dolores had intervened. "I think she may be sick. Let me take her to the clinic for a check-up. When she was at my house this happened twice and I was too tied down taking care of both of the children I couldn't take her then. You don't have to drive us. I'll take the bus."

Es glared at Dolores, "Don't interfere. She's my responsibility and I'm going to handle this. She resents me taking Rose's place and is just trying to get back at me. Maybe you'd better find a place of your own. Get upstairs, you're all wet. And don't put your good shorts on. We're not going to take you with us to supper tonight. You can stay home with your grandma and babysit Sam. I'm not going to put up with your bids for attention." Es was shouting by the time she finished the tirade.

After Melinda got up, she climbed the steps slowly. Her tongue was sore where she had bitten it. Es was still talking in a loud voice and directing her comments to Dolores. Melinda couldn't help hearing her tell grandma that she couldn't stand much more of this. Melinda wondered what "this" was.

Late that night Dolores had trouble sleeping. What could she do? If she told Doug she was planning to move out he might attempt to find a logical explanation. At the wedding Tilly had mentioned that perhaps Dolores would be happy moving in with her. Doug and Es had protested, saying she was needed. Now Dolores didn't feel as much needed as she felt in the way. Tomorrow she'd call Till and arrange for a long visit. Maybe after a few weeks Es would feel more comfortable about handling her responsibilities. Maybe Es was experiencing more problems than she admitted with the combined family and having a new baby. Dolores didn't want to add to the problem of the adjustment.

Till was delighted when she called. She was planning a trip to Canada in September and invited Dolores to come along. "It would be good," she said, "to have company."

The senior citizen group at the "Y" was sponsoring a bus trip to see the fall foliage. When Dolores asked how much it would cost, Till insisted on paying for both fares. Douglas seemed glad that his aunt was taking his mother. Es agreed with him.

The morning Till came to pick Dolores up, she was surprised that there were three suitcases waiting by the front door. "You can only take one large case with you on the bus and a carry-on."

"I've packed a few things extra to leave at your house. Some heavy winter things I might need later on. I may be staying with you for a while when we get back," Dolores explained.

By the time Tilly and Dolores returned from Canada, the sisters were feeling as close as they'd been as teenagers. On the trip Dolores had shared with Till much of the story of Rose and her experiences living with Es. Tilly encouraged Dolores to make a break and stay with Harry and her permanently.

Douglas seemed content to let his mother go. Esmirelda had mentioned how she was enjoying having the house to herself and although she never specifically told Doug how she had resented her mother-in-law's interference, it was obvious that although it meant a lot of extra work, she didn't miss Dolores.

Frequently Doug felt Es was too harsh in her discipline of Melinda but had stopped interfering after a few skirmishes about the way she handled Melinda's "black-outs". Obviously, Es's Latin temper was easily aroused and Doug felt the less he interfered the sooner Es would be able to feel comfortable handling Melinda.

He didn't believe that Melinda was deliberately "blacking-out" to get attention. When he had tried to explain that perhaps the adjustments to the new family were difficult, Es brushed his idea aside with a burst of maternal indignation. He did notice that the incidents were becoming more frequent and were lasting for longer periods of time.

Melinda was glad when school started again. She was glad to be in first grade. Sister Mary Frances put her in the front row. She put Charmain in one of the back rows on the other side of the room. When Charmain complained to her mother that the sister was giving Melinda special treatment, Es arrived at school and demanded that Charmain's seat be changed to the front also. Sister rearranged the seating. Despite Es's demands, she gave both girls a seat in the middle of class at opposite sides of the room.

Once in a while, Dolores and Till would stop by Douglas' to visit Melinda and Richard. When Dolores asked if the children could spend a weekend at Till's, Es readily agreed. Dolores missed the children and was delighted that she would have a chance to catch up on their progress. Richard was almost four and Melinda just six. At this age, just a few weeks made a difference.

When Tilly arrived the following Friday to pick up the children she was greeted at the door by Es.

"Richard will be ready in a minute. Melinda won't be coming. She's having one of her temper tantrums so I'm punishing her. Maybe she'll be better behaved and come some other time."

Till asked if she could see Melinda. Es told her that was impossible that she had put Melinda in the basement coal cellar and she wasn't letting her out until she has been there at least an hour. Es proudly announced this treatment was working and that Melinda hadn't "acted-up" for several weeks.

Reluctantly, Till drove off with Richard. By now Till knew that her sister's concerns about Melinda were justified. When she tried to discuss it with Dolores it did no good. Tilly decided to tell Douglas the next time she saw him.

Dolores didn't see either of the children until Thanksgiving. Harry had insisted that all the family go to the Livingston Hotel for Thanksgiving dinner. He'd worked there in the maintenance department and got a discount on meals. Sam was able to sit in a highchair and although the dining room was crowded, everyone tried to have a good time. Melinda sat next to her grandmother and complained of a headache. Es glared at her across the table.

"Complaining again! Couldn't wait to complain when you saw your grandma, could you? She complains all the time of her head . . . just trying to get attention."

Melinda smiled wanly. Dolores squeezed her hand under the table to let her know that she understood. Except for this brief outburst, the meal went well.

On Christmas morning, Doug invited Harry, Tilly and Dolores over to watch the children open their gifts. It was delightful watching the surprise on their faces as they unwrapped the packages that Santa had left under the tree. Dolores had bought a large doll with real hair for Melinda and a bike for Richard. She also had smaller gifts for Sam and Charmain. After all the packages were opened the children played on the floor for a while. Charmain reached over and picked up Melinda's new doll. This started a ruckus.

"Let Charmain play with your new doll," Es told Melinda.

"She'll ruin the hair like she did on her Annette doll you gave her for her birthday," Melinda protested.

"You're selfish," Charmain replied.

"It's her doll," Dolores joined in. "Give it back to Melinda, Charmain."

"Charmain, you just keep playing with that doll as long as you want," Es glared at Dolores. "Melinda needs to be taught to share."

"Well, just for a few minutes," Melinda looked appealingly at Doug for support.

Douglas wasn't about to take sides. He'd learned that Es wanted to handle the discipline of the children herself and that he only made things worse for his children if he interfered.

Charmain began to pull on the new doll's hair and rumple her clothing. She took off the doll's shoes and socks and stuffed them under the sofa. When she began telling Richard to run over the doll with his bike, Melinda burst into tears. Es jumped up and grabbed Melinda roughly by the arm. "Come with me. I'll teach you to not put on a scene to get attention. It's downstairs with you till you can behave better in front of company." As she was saying this she began dragging the limp child into the kitchen. Melinda didn't protest.

All of them could hear the bump, bump, bump as Es dragged Melinda down the basement steps. For just a brief moment the children were frozen. Since Charmain seemed to interpret this as permission to do anything with the doll, she grabbed it by the feet and swung it around and let it go crashing into the wall. The china head broke.

"Now see what you've done," Dolores exclaimed. She stood up and turned to Douglas.

"You'd better control this child, her mother is spoiling her rotten. Come on, Till and Harry, we're going home. Merry Christmas!" The last remark was said with a lot of sarcasm.

Dolores shrugged off Doug's help with her coat and his murmured apologies. Charmain sat smirking on the floor. Before they left, Dolores walked over and picked up the broken doll and all the broken pieces. She placed it in the shopping bag that had held all the packages when they arrived.

"Tell Melinda that I'll bring the doll back when it is fixed."

As the car pulled away from the house, Dolores started to cry. Douglas didn't seem to be able to take charge of the family or be aware of how badly Es was treating Melinda. Tilly glanced back at her sister, slumped in the rear seat. She knew how much Dolores had paid for the doll and how much she had hoped to please Melinda. Harry, who usually let both Till and Dolores converse for hours without interruption, started talking about the incident.

"Doug has got his hands full with that Spanish woman," he said. "He's letting her and her children rule the roost and it isn't fair. I didn't especially like Rose, but the children deserve better treatment. I bet there's no light in that coal cellar and she's going to let poor Melinda sit down there for hours. I think you're right, Dolores, there's something wrong with that girl. Did you see the way she went limp when Esmirelda grabbed her? It was all I could do to sit there and not interfere."

This only made the sobbing in the rear seat escalate. Tilly was surprised that Harry had voiced himself so strongly. It must have bothered him a lot. His prediction of Melinda's plight would come true, though none of them would know it for several weeks.

Snow was beginning to fall and the rest of the trip was

made in silence. All of them were thinking about the scene they had just left, the miserable little girl, and the broken doll.

The last week in January there was a knock on Dolores' bedroom door. She had just come up from supper and was sitting looking at the television Harry and Till had given her for Christmas. It was the nicest room Dolores had ever had. It was spacious with three large windows which overlooked the expansive backyard. The tiny rosebud wallpaper had matching drapes. The solid rose bedspread over the maple double bed made the room cheery even in the evening light. Dolores called out that the door was open.

One look at Doug when he opened the door and Dolores knew that he'd come looking for a favor. He'd had that hangdog look ever since he was a kid when he wanted her to do something for him.

"Nice of you to come visit. Haven't seen you since Christmas. How is everyone at your house? I've had a cold but been well otherwise. Not that you've bothered to call and ask. Have a seat." Dolores pointed to the straight chair opposite her recliner.

"I know I've been careless about keeping in touch. I've been given a promotion and been very busy. Lots of night work and weekends as well. The kids have been passing the chicken pox from one to another. Richard brought it home from school, then Charmain got it. Now Melinda and Sam are sick. Sam has it bad. All over his face and body. And he won't stop scratching. It's driving Es nuts. She's afraid that it will leave scars on his face like her brother has.

"That's why I've come over. My company wants me to go to Toledo for a week or so. This new promotion will mean that I have to travel a lot. Could you possibly come over and stay at the house at least until this bout of illness is over? Esmirelda is making a stink about my being away."

"Does she know you're over here asking me?" Dolores

raised her brow. "I didn't think she'd ever want me any place near the house after the scene she made when I brought the doll back two weeks ago. She said Melinda didn't deserve it and that I should trash it. It's still in that closet. If I go over, the doll goes with me." Dolores pointed to the walk-in closet on the far side of the room.

"Es is sorry about the doll. You know her temper gets the best of her sometimes. At least she's a kind person and good to the children. I have no complaints. As a matter of fact it was her idea that I come over and ask you if you'd do this as a favor to both of us."

"Did she say I could bring the doll? I'm not coming without it. When do you want me to come?"

"Tomorrow. I have to leave early the following morning. It would be better if you started tomorrow night since my flight is at seven A.M. Of course you can bring the doll. I said Es was sorry. I could pick you up after supper tomorrow, if that's okay?" Doug's voice had acquired a pleading tone. It reminded Dolores of when he'd beg to go sledding although all his clothing was wet.

"You don't give much notice, do you? I suppose it'll be all right. I'll miss helping out at the church bazaar at the end of the week. How long did you say you'd be gone?"

"Hopefully it will be only about ten days. A plant out there has purchased some of the equipment I engineered and I will have to stay until they install it and have it running. You can come home when Sam is better, I'm sure. If he's like Richard it won't be more than a few days."

Dolores sat for what seemed to Doug a long time before answering. The television was still on, although Dolores had turned off the sound. Three commercials later Dolores replied.

"I'll go for your sake. Just make sure before you pick me up tomorrow that Es knows I'm bringing the doll and I won't expect any guff about it after I get there."

"Gee, Ma, I'm sure it will be just fine," Doug smiled.

After a bit of small talk, Doug left. He was more relieved than he'd allowed his mother to see. He'd never suspected such a jealous scene from Es when he announced that he would be going out of town for a few weeks. She had interpreted all the extra overtime he'd been working as an indication of an affair he was having and that this was a romantic interlude he'd planned. After she explained how Amerillo, her first husband, had been unfaithful, Doug had understood. Nevertheless, she seemed frightened at being left alone. Perhaps she had suggested Dolores as a hedge against his roving while away. She'd almost said as much when she lightly suggested that he certainly wouldn't look at another woman when his mother was helping to take care of the children. As though one thing had anything to do with the other.

He was glad that Ma would be there while he was away. He hadn't told her but he suspected that once she arrived Es would find some excuse to keep her until he returned. Es had never admitted it but when Ma had been there it had given Es time to run around during the day without dragging the baby along. She was beginning to complain that they never went out at night because they couldn't find a reliable babysitter.

Dolores was pleasantly surprised at the welcome she got when she arrived the following evening. Esmirelda had moved Charmain into her room so that Dolores could sleep in the bedroom with Melinda.

Es said she was glad to see how well the doll had been repaired and went upstairs with Dolores to see that she got settled and even woke Melinda to show her the doll.

Melinda's face was covered with pox marks. When Dolores put her hand on her forehead it felt hot. She barely opened her eyes to glance at the doll. She gave a sleepy smile at her grandmother and immediately drifted back to sleep.

44

"Has she been drinking?" Dolores asked.

"She doesn't want anything. She hardly ate anything all today or yesterday. Once in a while I try to get her to drink some juice but she just pushes it away."

"I'd better give her a sponge bath. She's terribly hot. Has the doctor been in to see the children?" Dolores persisted. As long as she was there to help with the sick she might as well start.

"Leave her alone," Es remarked. "Nobody calls the doctor for chicken pox. Richard and Charmain snapped out of it by the third day. She'll be all right in the morning. Come on down. I've saved some dessert for you. That lemon tart you like so well."

Both Richard and Charmain seemed happy to see Dolores. They came and sat on either side of her on the couch and asked for a story. Charmain apologized for breaking the doll. Dolores knew that the child had been told to do it but accepted her apology with a hug. When both of them were sent to bed, she also excused herself. Es was overjoyed to have someone take care of the bedtime routine upstairs. Sam was being cranky and taking all of her attention.

"I certainly appreciate you coming and taking over like this particularly since Doug is going away," she cooed at Dolores as she went upstairs.

As soon as she could, Dolores returned to bathe Melinda with some cool water. She sponged the sleeping child and changed her wet top sheet. Then she sat in the semi-darkness and watched while Melinda slept. After a while Dolores began to doze. It was around one o'clock when Melinda began moaning and talking in her sleep.

"Please let me out of this dark place. I'll be good. I have to go to the bathroom. You'll be mad if I wet my pants like last time. Ouch, don't kick me like that. I'll stay over in the corner."

Dolores roused herself. She was still sitting on the rocker. She stood up and walked over to the bed. Melinda sat straight up. Her eyes were still closed but she continued to beg to be let out of the "dark place."

"Melinda it's me, Grandma," Dolores said, putting her hand lightly on the child's arm. "Wake up darling. You're dreaming. Everything is going to be all right. You've had a fever but I think it is going down."

Melinda woke up with a start and grabbed hold of Dolores around the waist. "Don't leave me. Please take care of me. I've missed you so much. Did you get my doll fixed? Daddy told me you would."

"I brought it with me. We woke you up hours ago to show it to you but I think you were too sleepy. How do you feel? Can I get you something to drink? You have to drink a lot to make the fever go away. I'll go get the doll and you can hold it while I go downstairs and get you some nice cold juice."

Dolores put the doll in Melinda's arms and tiptoed out of the room and down the steps. By the time she returned she had to wake Melinda again so that she could make her drink the apple juice.

*   *   *

By the following Monday both of the sick children were feeling better. Although they both had red marks, the daily baths and lotion were controlling the itching. Es had been bending over backwards to make Dolores feel welcome.

"Tomorrow I think Melinda can go back to school. Most of her red marks are disappearing. Sister allowed Charmain to come back when she looked like Melinda does. Since most of the children in the class have had chicken pox already I suppose she doesn't care. The doctor says that the only time they are contagious is before they get spots anyway. I'm running low on almost everything. Could you keep an eye on Sam when he naps today, while I go to the supermarket?"

Dolores was happy to be helpful. She had hoped that when both the children were better she might return home. It looked as though Es needed her support. "Sure, just stop by Till's and get me a few dresses while you're out. I guess you'll want me to stay for a bit more. Sam has slobbered all over the two dresses that I brought along and they'll have to go to the cleaners. I forgot babies were so messy or I'd have brought some of my wash dresses."

The next week went by swiftly. Doug called to say he'd be able to be home in a few days sooner than he'd expected and by the time he returned, everything was running smoothly.

On the ride back to Till's in the car, Doug thanked his mother again for her help. He'd brought her a small vase of artificial flowers from Toledo that would just match the wallpaper in her room. Dolores was touched that he had remembered.

"If I have to go away on a trip again maybe you'll come over and stay again?" Doug questioned as he left her off at the curb.

"We'll see, just give me a little more notice next time. I've gotten some social activities of my own, you know. If it will help out I'll try to come." Dolores didn't want to give cart blanche acceptance to the invitation. She wanted Doug not to take advantage of her, even though she hadn't minded helping.

5

Sister Mary Frances

In the over thirty years that Sister Mary Frances had been teaching first grade, she had never encountered a child with the abilities that Melinda Dixon demonstrated. Sister knew that the child had a photographic memory from the way she could find any passage that the class was assigned. Not only did she find it first, but without looking could "recite" whole paragraphs perfectly.

It wasn't only in reading that Melinda excelled, her math and drawing abilities were superior as well. Early in the year, Sister had made the mistake of mentioning this to Esmirelda, not realizing that this mother was extremely partial to her own natural daughter. Es had instantly asked that Melinda be assigned to assist Charmain during class. When she had been told that this would be disruptive to the other children, Es had gone off in a huff and complained to the principal about the "uncooperative" nun.

Father Dunne had been understanding and supportive of his first-grade teacher. This had initiated a letter to the Monsignor and a threat to have both girls removed from the school. The ensuing discussion resulted in having both girls removed from the room during recess and Melinda was given time to help Charmain with her math. Of course, both girls resented losing recess and Charmain stubbornly resisted any help her stepsister tried to give her.

Looking at the girls sitting at their desks, Sister occasionally was struck by the contrast they made. Melinda with curly blonde hair, tall, slim, pale and studious. Charmain with straight black hair, short, plump and carefree. Charmain had attracted a group of girls that chased after the boys in the yard at recess and teased the other girls. Sister's suspicion of this was confirmed since once Charmain was removed at recess time most of the teasing stopped. Perhaps Charmain observed her mother's managing and was following suit.

After the January epidemic of chicken pox, the class started making decorations for the Valentine party, a school-wide traditional fete to which parents and the community were invited. Melinda had been given the job of designing a large banner to go across the front of the stage. Since her skills were so superior, Sister allowed her to go to the third grade room in the afternoons to have the older children work on the decoration project. Once again Esmirelda arrived at school, protesting. It was clear that Charmain had complained that Melinda was being given special treatment. After trying to reason with Es, Sister finally gave in and allowed Charmain to go along with Melinda.

Tuesday afternoon, February tenth started out as a stressful day. At chapel in the morning Charmain had been whispering and was sent to the principal's office. After sitting on a bench for an hour during recess time, the secretary had sent Charmain to the room with a note saying that Father Dunne was delayed at a funeral and that perhaps Charmain could be able to come to see him after school.

Charmain came back from lunch with a note from her mother stating that it would be impossible for Charmain to stay after school as she had a dentist appointment. Sister doubted that the excuse was valid but was hesitant to get into another confrontation with Esmirelda. Father Dunne would have to handle this on his own. Sister did tell Charmain that she wouldn't be able to sing in the chorus unless she could stay in the room and practice instead of going with Melinda to the third-grade room.

The decision was painful. Sister knew that Melinda had such a sweet voice and had learned all the words to the songs so quickly that she didn't need to practice. Charmain couldn't remember the words. With only three days of preparation left, to put this ultimatum to Charmain seemed only reasonable.

Sister hadn't reckoned on Charmain's jealousy. She said she would rather go along with Melinda. Off both girls went, Charmain tripping Melinda as they entered Sister May Jane's third-grade room. When one of the hearts she had been trying to cut out ripped, Charmain poked the scissors at Melinda and kicked her hard on the leg.

Melinda felt her head start spinning and knew that she would fall as she started shaking and seeing the room going round and round as everything turned black.

One of the boys screamed as Melinda accidentally knocked him down, taking him with her as she fell. Sister May rushed over and looked down at the trembling child. All the other children came and stared at the quivering body. Melinda's tongue was protruding and she had bitten it when she fell. A trickle of blood was coming down her chin.

"Don't pay any attention to her," Charmain yelled. "She's always doing this at home to get attention."

Sister May Jane hesitated, after all, Charmain seemed to have observed Melinda's behavior before. When the shaking stopped and Melinda still lay unresponsive on the floor, Sister sent Joseph to the office to get Father Dunne. "Tell him to call for an ambulance."

In five minutes Father Dunne and Miss Turner, his secretary, were kneeling beside the prostrate body. Miss Turner took charge. She'd been an Army nurse and knew how to handle most emergencies at the school. She started out by loosening Melinda's uniform and removing her shoes and tights. As she rolled the tights down over Melinda's thighs, Shelia Turner gasped. The entire area over her thighs was covered with bruises. There was hardly an area that wasn't black and blue. When she looked up, the children were staring at the unconscious child.

"Charmain, can you tell me how many times this has happened before?" Sister May inquired as she herded the class out of the room.

"Lots of times. Not this bad, though. Mom always tells us to ignore her, that she's trying to get her own way. If she stays quiet for a while it will go away. You'll see. Mom will be mad if you send her to the hospital. One time Dad tried to call the doctor when this happened and Mom had a fit."

After the children and Father Dunne left, Shelia took off her jacket and tried to keep Melinda warm. She gently moved her out of the large puddle of urine that had accumulated under her body. Father returned shortly with the news that Douglas Dixon was out of the office but that Esmirelda had protested that it wasn't necessary since Melinda frequently had "spells," but finally agreed to meet them at Dimsdale General.

On the ride to the hospital in the ambulance, Father Dunne talked to Sister Mary Frances, who had requested that she go along when she heard what had happened. It was near the end of the day and Shelia was frequently asked to substitute in an emergency.

"Did you see the bruises all over her thighs?" Father asked. "Do you think that she's been mistreated by Mrs. Dixon?"

"I don't know. That woman has been giving Charmain favorite treatment all year. You know that. Could she be this cruel?" Melinda stirred and the ambulance attendant again took her blood pressure.

"Hello, Melinda, can you open your eyes and look at me?" Sister bent across the aisle and took the limp hand.

"She'll come out of it gradually, Sister," the attendant said. "We'll be in the hospital soon. Don't be anxious. We've taken care of many seizure patients before. She won't be able to answer you for a while yet."

The siren stopped blasting as they rolled into the emergency entrance of the hospital. Quickly and efficiently the ambulance crew extended the legs on the stretcher and pushed Melinda through the automatic doors. Once inside they quickly slid her onto the emergency room table and departed.

A nurse began taking Melinda's clothing off. Sister Mary Frances had gone along and stood watching. Father Dunne was still outside giving some information to the desk clerk. Mrs. Dixon was still not at the hospital. The nurse looked up at the small, rotund, black-garbed figure and raised her eyebrows.

"Do you know anything about this child? Do you know how long she's been having seizures? Look at all these bruises on her torso. Has she ever complained about being beaten at home?"

Sister looked at Melinda's thin naked body. All over her chest, abdomen and thighs were ugly blue, purple and green bruises. Sister Mary's stomach tightened. She hoped she wouldn't be sick and add to the nurse's problems.

Avoiding the nurses eyes, she finally swallowed hard and answered. "This is one of my pupils. She has never had a seizure in school but her half-sister told us that she has had some at home. I don't know how she got the bruises. When her parents arrive maybe you can ask them. Poor thing. She's so talented and brilliant. Do you think she'll be well enough to be at our Valentine presentation on Saturday?"

Her question was ignored, for an intern had arrived and

was making a preliminary examination. Melinda was awakening and he began asking her questions as well as directing the nurse to call for the portable X-ray machine and a lab technician to take blood.

Esmirelda came bustling in, carrying Sam, who was crying. "What's the matter? Did this child try to get attention at school with one of her darn fool acts? She doesn't need a doctor, she needs a good beating. She'll be okay in an hour or so as soon as she sees that this acting out won't do her any good."

The intern whirled around and faced Esmirelda angrily. "Are you this child's mother? You'll have to get that crying child out of here. I'll talk to you later. Just go out to the desk and sign the permission forms for us to take care of her!" he shouted.

"I'll do no such thing. She doesn't need any 'care.' I'll take her home and make sure she doesn't do this in school again."

"Sister," the intern turned to Mary Frances, "please take this woman out of this room. Please convince her to sign the forms. It's obvious that the child needs hospitalization. She's malnourished, mistreated, and has a serious seizure disorder which has been long neglected. We'll have to do extensive testing and regulate medication before she can go home."

Esmirelda's face turned pale at this explanation. She followed the Sister out into the waiting room and without further protest signed the consent forms at the desk and gave them the necessary information about the insurance.

There was a hustle as technicians and equipment went in and out the door to the room where Melinda had been taken. In the waiting room Esmirelda handed Sam over to Dolores. She had stopped to pick him up on the way to the hospital. The call from Father Dunne hadn't alarmed her. She'd been more annoyed than worried but knew that if Melinda had to

53

stay at the hospital for any length of time that she'd have to hurry home to be there when Charmain and Richard came home. Dolores had readily volunteered to stay at the hospital until Doug came to take Melinda home.

"I can't see why you weren't alarmed at Melinda's seizures before this," Sister threw caution to the wind. Despite her previous encounters with Esmirelda, the situation seemed to merit a direct approach. How dare this mother ignore such an obvious medical problem?

"What seizures? Melinda has been acting out for months. Whenever she didn't get her way or wanted attention she'd lie on the floor and pretend to shake and not hear us. I'd take her down to the coal cellar and let her be for a while and she'd always snap out of it. That doctor's just trying to scare me."

Esmirelda belligerently refused to acknowledge that she'd been negligent. Particularly in front of both Father Dunne and Sister Mary Frances. She felt both of them had been favoring Melinda since she started school.

When Doug was in Toledo, Dolores hadn't questioned that Es always insisted on bathing Melinda. She had only seen Melinda's arms and legs the night she had given her a sponge bath. There might have been a few bruises she hadn't noticed in the dim light. While Melinda was sick, Es had always made a big fuss about dressing Melinda.

Dolores reflected on another thing. Melinda was a slow eater. Although she always ate everything on her plate, Melinda had never asked for seconds. Es served skimpy platters for everyone with the excuse that the children were picky and she didn't want to waste food. Richard always asked for seconds and thirds and so did Charmain. Was the fact that Melinda didn't ask because all the food had been consumed or that she'd been intimidated previously by Es?

It was nearly nine when she saw Doug coming out of the

elevator. He was followed by a burly police officer. The officer pointed down the hall toward the nurses' station. Dolores got up and rushed after them. They were standing at the desk before she caught up with them. "Doug, where have you been? I've been waiting a long time for you to get here. Melinda is going to be fine."

"Hi, Ma. I was on business in Sellersville and just got on the road for home when I was stopped by the State Patrol. They told me what happened. Thanks for waiting. Where's Es?"

"She went home to take care of the other children. Maybe she was hoping we'd be back by now. I haven't had any money to call."

The nurse on duty, who had been conversing with the police officer, turned to Doug. "Come with me, Mr. Dixon. Melinda is asleep but we are going to wake her now that you are here."

Doug followed the nurse. The policeman turned to Dolores. "You'd better stay out here, Ma'am. I'm sure they'll let you see your grandchild soon."

It alarmed Dolores when the policeman followed Doug into her room. *Why were the police here? Why had he accompanied Doug up to the hospital? Was something wrong with Melinda they weren't telling her?*

Nurse Betty Grace shook Melinda's foot to wake her. The small body that lay in a fetal position unwound and looked around the partially lit room. Her focus centered on her father and she let out a delighted squeal. "Daddy, you came! At first I thought I was back in the coal cellar but when I saw you I knew I was someplace else. Where am I? What happened to me? I remember being at school this afternoon."

"You're in a hospital, dear," Doug reached over and smoothed the rumpled golden curls. "I came as fast as I could. I won't be able to stay long, but Grandma is outside and I'm sure that everyone here is going to take good care of you and make you well." He glanced up at the intravenous bottle and turned to the nurse. "Why is she hooked up to that bottle?"

"Your daughter is malnourished and dehydrated. We will keep feeding her extra nutrients for a while."

Melinda turned her head to look at Betty and then noticed the policeman who was standing behind the nurse. "Why's he here?" she asked.

"I brought your father here. We're holding him until there is a hearing tomorrow to determine whether we're going to put him in jail," Officer Hartled stated brusquely.

Melinda sat up and grabbed Doug around the waist. Her face looked beseechingly up at the officer. "My dad is a good man. He's never done anything wrong in his whole life. You can't tell me he has. Tell him it's a mistake, Daddy."

"No mistake, honey. They think I'm at fault for not reporting your illness sooner. I think I can explain it to the magistrate. Don't you worry. Everything will be hunky dory. You just concentrate on getting better fast so that you can come to the party on Saturday. I'm looking forward to seeing that banner you made at school."

"Gotta go." Officer Hartley nodded toward the door and put his hand against Doug's back, pushing him in that direction.

"I'll go tell your grandma to come see you," Doug bent down and gave Melinda a gentle hug. He reluctantly went out the door.

"I have to go with Officer Hartley, Ma," Doug explained to Dolores who was standing outside the door to Melinda's room. He reached into his pocket and took out a few crumpled bills. "Here, get a taxi. I'll call you tomorrow.

"Don't worry. There's some kind of problem. The hospital is accusing me of neglect and I'll have to go to a hearing tomorrow. Until then I have to go with the officer."

"Will you need a lawyer? I can call that friend of Harry's that helped him with his income tax. How can we help?" Dolores frowned at the officer. He was pushing Doug down the hall toward the elevator.

"No, I have to explain everything, that's all." As both men neared the elevator the doors opened and Father Dunne, followed by Sister Mary Frances, emerged.

"I'm glad to see that you got here, Mr. Dixon," Sister said. She smiled and then, looking at the policeman, wrinkled her brow. "Is Melinda feeling better? I hope she's not taken a turn for the worse."

"No," Doug patted the Sister's hand. "You can go in to see her with Ma. She's awake and I know she'd like to see you. Thank you for coming, Father. Excuse me, I have to be going."

The officer had been holding the door open and they both got into the elevator and the doors closed.

"But . . . ," Dolores couldn't ask any more questions.

"Wasn't that nice of the policeman to bring Douglas to the hospital?" Sister commented. One look at the distress on Dolores' face stopped her from making further remarks. Father Dunne was striding down to the nurses' station. He arrived in time to overhear Betty Grace's directions to her assistant.

"For a child with so many injuries and a seizure disorder I'm amazed at how alert she seems. She'll have to stay here for a long time, however. Her red blood count is low and we'll have to get her electrolytes balanced as well as start her on some seizure medication. Did you know she'd had two broken ribs recently? You'll have to check her vital signs every hour."

"Good evening, Father. Are you here to see the Dixon girl?"

Father Dunne turned away from the desk as Betty pointed across the hall to indicate Melinda's room. He joined

Dolores and Sister as they all entered the darkened room. The nightlight over the bed shone on Melinda's sleeping face. Another child lay sleeping in the far bed.

"I thought Doug said she was awake," Dolores was disappointed. "She must be all tired out. Let's not disturb her. I'll just say a prayer before we go." Father Dunne softly said the prayer for the sick and both women stood with bowed heads.

"Amen," a small voice said.

"Melinda, we don't want to wake you. It is late at night and you should be getting your rest. We just came to see if you were feeling better," Father Dunne said softly.

"I'm glad you woke me up. Daddy was here a little while ago with a policeman. The policeman said something about Daddy going to jail. That scared me. Hello, Sister. I'm sorry I didn't get the banner finished. I'll come in tomorrow and it will be all done in time for the party."

"I'm afraid that you won't be able to come to school tomorrow, Melinda," Father Dunne explained. "Don't concern yourself about the banner. Your plans were so well made I'm sure Sister Mary will be able to help the children finish it. You concentrate on getting well . . .

"Turn over and go back to sleep and don't worry your little head about anything. I love you and I'll be back tomorrow to see you when you are more awake. We are sure that the doctors and nurses will take good care of you." Dolores smoothed the sheet over the blanket and kissed Melinda on the forehead. Melinda's eyes closed and her body curled itself into a tight ball as they walked quietly back into the hall.

"Can I drive you home?" the Father asked Dolores.

"I'm sorry, I never introduced myself," Dolores extended her hand to the priest. "I'm Melinda's grandmother, Douglas' mother. It was good of you to take time to come back to check on her tonight. I feel you've done enough. I can take a taxi. I live quite a distance from your parish. I'm in St. Madeline's parish across town."

"It isn't that far. Besides I want to talk to you about what Melinda said about Douglas going to jail, I'd be happy to go to the hearing if you'd like." By now all three were in the elevator and they walked out the door to the parking lot.

"All I know is that Doug said he was being accused of neglect and that I didn't have to get a lawyer because it was just a misunderstanding. I don't want to accuse her, but if anyone has neglected that child I do think Esmirelda is to blame." Dolores spoke with guarded tones. She was hesitant to reveal to the priest some of what she'd witnessed.

She followed Father Dunne as he walked toward his car. He held the door open and she got into the front seat of the black Plymouth. Sister Mary Frances opened the rear door and got into the back seat.

"I've noticed that Melinda's stepmother seems to favor Charmain. Both girls have such different capabilities. The mother has been displaying her protectiveness all year."

Sister didn't elaborate on her run-ins with Esmirelda. Perhaps the grandmother would be able to figure out that she'd been observing preferential treatment of Charmain on Es's part.

"What street do you live on?" asked the Father. "I still would be glad to help if I can. Let me know if you want me to show up at Doug's hearing. Maybe I can call the precinct to find out when it will be held."

"Thank you, Father. I live at 697 Elm Street with my sister and her husband. I do appreciate this ride. It isn't always easy to get a taxi this late at night. If you show up at the court when Doug has his hearing, I'd appreciate it. I suppose that Esmirelda will want to go too. If you call her, tell her I'll be happy to babysit Sam."

The remainder of the ride was in silence. Each one of the passengers was deep in thought. Father Dunne pondered over the conversation he'd overheard concerning Melinda's condition. Surely Melinda had been suffering from neglect. Sister Mary Frances replayed some of the scenes with Esmirelda. Sister felt guilty for not seeing the complexity of the problem. She could have tried to help Melinda sooner. Dolores was engrossed in reviewing the events of the day. Suddenly she felt excessively weak and realized that except for a small breakfast, she'd had no food. As the car came to a stop on Elm Street she was relieved to be home. A sandwich and a cup of tea would be welcome.

*   *   *

"I can't believe it!" Sister Mary Frances stared in disbelief at the bowed head of Father Dunne across the desk in the school office. It was a pleasant room with dark wood paneling, pictures, and a large crucifix hung directly behind the desk. The fading sunlight through the windows was brightening the room with reflections of snow, which was falling in billows.

"None of our children in this school have ever been sent to foster care. None of our parents, except for that Mr. Rafferty years ago, have ever had to go to jail. And for neglect at that. How did Judge Halloran arrive at such a decision? Why didn't Mr. Dixon speak against his wife? Are you the one who has to break it to Melinda?"

Father Dunne raised his head. "This has been a devastating experience for all of us. I had to sit at that hearing this morning, helpless. Mrs. Dixon didn't even show up. Even after she promised on the phone last night. The trial won't be until next month but after listening to Halloran I doubt that Doug has a chance of bail. He went on and on about how these were Doug's children and his responsibility alone. Somehow Halloran even knew about their mother's murder and mentioned that was a mitigating circumstance in Doug's responsibility. Then when he demanded that the children be removed from the home and placed in foster care I didn't know what to think."

"Charmain too?" Sister raised her eyebrows.

"No. Both Charmain and the baby will be staying with Mrs. Dixon. I suppose from what we've been observing they should be safe. Perhaps there was a lot of resentment about having to take care of stepchildren. I'll have to go see her. I guess someone from family court will show up sometime tomorrow to take Richard for placement. Sometimes this job has more sorrows than I like."

"Do you want me to go with you to the hospital to see Melinda?" Sister asked. "Maybe when Mr. Dixon goes home he'll tell his wife and you won't have to go see her."

"They've set bail so high I doubt that he'll be able to make it. I think he'll be in jail until the trial. Come along with me to the hospital if you like. Melinda will be there for a long time if what I overheard last night is true. I won't tell her yet. She should recover a bit before I tell her."

6

Dolly

The two months since Richard had gone to live with Dolly had gone by swiftly. She watched as he would run impatiently to the window to see if the car which was bringing Melinda from the hospital had arrived. Richard had adjusted to the placement well. His outgoing nature had made it easy for him to find his niche in the Erfer household.

Besides her own two boys, Bill and Donald, there were two foster children living with Dolly and Chris in their roomy bungalow. When Melinda arrived, she would be the second girl. The social worker had explained about Melinda's medical problems and medication needs. There had been enough publicity about the case that Dolly knew about Doug being sentenced to two years.

Shirley joined Richard at the window. She was seven and a half. Her mom was in the hospital recovering from a serious operation. Except that Shirley sometimes cried for her mother, she had made the adjustment to living with the Erfers well. It would probably be a few months until her mother would be able to take care of her. In the meantime, since she was a quiet child, she added little extra work for Dolly.

Dolly was worried about Tinker, the other foster child. He was the oldest. At twelve he was beginning to act out not only here in the house but at school and on the street as well. When he'd first arrived, Dolly thought he'd make a fine playmate for Donald, who was eleven. Tinker ignored Donald most of the time except when he tried to get him to take part in one of his escapades.

Tinker's father and mother had been separated and neither one of them wanted him. After he had set fire to a shed and a field, the court had sent him to foster placement.

Only an hour ago Dolly had caught him teasing Richard about his "sick" sister and his "jailbird" dad. Richard didn't understand why Tinker kept taunting him and calling his family names, but he knew by now not to respond. Tinker had twisted his arm so many times that Richard had begun to do anything to avoid the bigger boy.

"They're here! They're here!" Richard sang out. He ran to the porch door and opened it. Although it was a bitterly cold April day he ran down the steps and grabbed his sister as she got out of the car. The social worker hurried them both into the house. She carried only a small suitcase with her.

"I'm so glad to see you, Melinda," Richard was holding her hand although she was trying to take off her coat. "You must have been awful sick. It was a long time before they said you could come home. This is Mrs. Erfer. She's nice. She'll take good care of you when you have a spell. And this is Shirley. You're going to share a room with her. It'll be right next to Billy's and my room. Come on I'll show it to you right now."

Richard was pulling on Melinda's arm, taking her in the direction of the center hall and the back bedrooms.

"Wait a minute, Richard," Dolly said. She helped Melinda off with her coat. She was surprised that Melinda was wearing a school uniform. "I'm glad you're going to be here with us. Richard has been looking forward to seeing you for hours."

"Let them go," Kelly Anderson, the social worker, smiled at the obvious joy of the children who had been separated for the past two months. Melinda, Richard and Shirley ran down the hall. Even after they had gone into the bedroom, their excited babbling could be heard in the living room.

"Can we go into the kitchen?" Kelly requested. "I would like to talk. By the way here are only a few things that I brought with me for Melinda. I'll leave you some money so that you can buy her some school clothing and whatever else you think she needs. I know she'll be going to public school with the others so she'll have to have some more clothes. Since we've had no cooperation from her stepmother, I couldn't get any clothing from there."

Dolly brought up her problems with Tinker. Kelly said, "I'd like to suggest a different placement for him." At twelve, boys were hard to place. She knew that she'd have to try to keep him with the Erfers as long as possible.

Kelly had been working for Dimsdale Child Welfare for twelve years. At forty-five, she looked dowdy and worn. Her hair was beginning to gray and she no longer made any attempt at make-up. Although she was tall, her posture was stooped and a bit of arthritis made her limp.

As the city had grown in size, so had the problems. The size of her case load had increased monthly. When she had first started to work at the agency there had been few court referrals. Now she hated trying to work out solutions for already abused and abandoned children. No matter how good the foster home, the children needed more help than either the foster parents or the agency could supply.

The Erfers were one of her best homes and obviously not trying to make extra income at the expense of their foster children. Over the past six years she had placed nine children with them. Some of them for only few weeks and some, like Richard and Melinda, would be there a long time. Dolly Erfer was a loving, understanding woman. Much younger than Kelly. She had had Donald when she was only nineteen and shortly after came Billy. Then she discovered it was impossible to have the large family that both she and Chris had wanted. It was then she had first contacted child welfare. Dolly had never complained about a child before, so Kelly left the house with much to think about.

Waving good-bye to Kelly from the window, Dolly turned to see Tinker put something in his pocket. Not wanting another scene, Dolly hurried down the hall to see how Melinda was settling in. To her surprise when she entered the bedrooms, he saw Shirley, who was always withdrawn, bouncing up and down on her bed hugging a small pink bunny.

"I'm glad to have a roommate," Shirley smiled. "Melinda said I could have the rabbit she brought home from the hospital. I need something to take to bed with me. Isn't he cute?"

This was the first time that Shirley had expressed any desires. Since she had come, she seemed to accept what was given with no questions, but no requests either. Dolly had never thought that she might need a cuddly toy to sleep with at her age. Maybe having Melinda would make it easier for Shirley. She hoped that Melinda would also find Shirley a good temporary sister. Melinda was staring at Shirley, trying to decide what kind of a person she would be sharing the room with.

Shirley was not as tall as Melinda was, although she said she was seven and a half. Melinda's birthday would be in July when she'd be seven. Shirley had long, brown, braided hair and big brown eyes that seemed to follow you wherever you went.

The room seemed to be decorated especially for little girls. The furniture was painted pink and there were frilly bedspreads and curtains to match. Over in the corner there was a large open toy chest and a small table and chairs with a set of dishes waiting for a tea party. Most importantly, there was a doll house. It looked as though no one had played with it for a long time, because the furniture was placed just so in all the rooms. Dolly had made sure that since she wasn't going to have girls of her own she would enjoy giving pleasure to the girls she took care of temporarily.

"We'll be having supper in about an hour, Melinda. Do you want to come in the kitchen with me and watch while I cook?"

"Maybe I can help. I always helped Grandma. I can cut up vegetables and break up the lettuce for salad. Sometimes grandma would let me help make a cake. I'm good at breaking eggs."

Melinda followed Dolly down the hall. Richard tagged along and Shirley ignored the invitation to join them and went to watch television with the boys.

While they were together preparing supper, Melinda hedged when Dolly started asking her about her family. During her stay in the hospital the only one to come visit was Dolores, the priest and Sister. She had had to stay in bed for the first few weeks but after that she went to the playroom on the pediatric floor and played with the other children.

She had one experience answering questions that she didn't want to repeat. A tall angry man in a dark blue suit had come to her room one day while she was still in bed. He had asked her a lot of questions about her father and Esmirelda. She had told him about not remembering anything when she passed out except that she frequently awakened in the coal cellar. At times she would have a headache or feel sore all over. Many times her tongue would be swollen. After she woke up, she recalled, she would seem to have been in the cellar for hours because when she was let out it would be dark and after dinner.

The man seemed angry that she couldn't remember, and kept asking who put her in and who took her out of the cellar.

He finally went away and a week later, Grandma told her that her Dad wouldn't be able to come see her. She wondered why Esmirelda and Charmain didn't come, but she didn't ask. From habit she blamed this desertion on being a bad girl. She had been told this so often that she believed it.

"You're going to be a fine helper," Dolly commented as Melinda placed the vegetable peelings in the garbage pail with no instructions. She reached down and gave Melinda a hug. Melinda backed away. She didn't know if she could trust Dolly yet.

The following morning, Dolly hurried through her chores. All the other children went to school so Melinda followed Dolly around and helped fold some of the small items as they came out of the dryer. By eleven they were on their way toward the shopping center to purchase some school clothing. Melinda was surprised that Dolly encouraged her to pick out some pastel colors and blouses with ruffles. Esmirelda had always said she didn't want anything that would be in the wash too often.

By the time they stopped for a bite to eat at Woolworth's some of Melinda's mistrust had begun to wear off. While they were eating, instead of a barrage of questions, Dolly began telling Melinda stories about what she had wanted when she was a little girl. Melinda was fascinated, for to look at this homely, unadorned woman she would have never guessed that Dolly had the heart of a romantic. Dolly mentioned how much she had liked reading about the knights and kings and queens and how in her heart of hearts she would have liked to go to Hollywood and be in the movies.

Finally some of what she was saying made Melinda recognize that she too was drawn to the fantasy world. She liked books that told stories about wonderful magical things. Her favorite was Cinderella. But most of all Melinda was fascinated by stories about the world of the circus. There had been one long story the nun had read her about a girl who rode standing on the back of a pony. Sometimes she would dream that she was that girl who wore pretty pink tights and a sequined jacket, like the picture in the book.

On the way home in the 1953 Cadillac that had a bashed-in side door, Melinda slid closer on the seat to Dolly. Dolly reached over and patted her on the hand.

"We had fun this morning, didn't we? Don't worry, Melinda, I know you may take some time to get used to living with Chris and me, but until your dad can come and take care of you and Richard, we are happy to have you as part of our family. I always wanted a little girl but God told me after I had my two boys that I'd have to borrow some and take good care of them instead."

Little did either of them suspect that the future for both of them would be a lot different than they hoped. The comforting words brought the first tears to Melinda's eyes that she had had since she'd been taken to the hospital. They rolled down her cheeks and her body shook with silent sobs. She reached up to brush them away and Dolly brought the car to the curb so she could reach over and comfort the little girl.

Although the hospital had managed to restore Melinda to better health, Dolly was shocked when she embraced her. She was little more than skin and bones. Instead of the bear hug Dolly was accustomed to giving, she restrained herself for fear that this fragile body couldn't take it.

For the remainder of the school term, Melinda accompanied all the children to the nearby elementary school, which went up to grade eight. Except for three occasions, Melinda's seizure medication had kept her well. Gradually she began to eat better also and the thinness of her face and body filled out. She was still reported to be undernourished by the school nurse when she was measured and weighed in late May. Not only had she grown two and a half inches since September, her weight had increased by thirteen pounds. Dolly hoped by the fall she would be up to normal weight for her height.

When Melinda had her first seizure one Saturday morning, Dolly had been surprised by the reaction of the other children. All of them except for Tinker and Richard had rushed out of the room, even though their favorite Showboat Sam was on the television. Richard had knelt down and rubbed his sister's hands.

"Don't worry," he said to Dolly. "She'll wake up soon. You don't have to kick her like Charmain did. You don't have to put her in the coal cellar."

Tinker still sat with his eyes glued on the T.V. but Dolly knew he was listening. It took only a few minutes until Melinda began to stir. Tinker came over and stared at her.

"What's the matter with her? I'd kick her too. She's probably mad because I poked her at school."

"She has epilepsy. That's why I give her those pills every morning and evening," Dolly explained. She was aware of the animosity that existed between Melinda and Tinker. He had tried his best to tease her when she had first arrived and Melinda had ignored him. Unlike Richard, she failed to respond to insults about her family. Even when Tinker called her father a "jailbird" she had merely made a face at him and turned her back. What did strike Dolly as worrying was his callous remarks about kicking an unconscious child.

Despite knowing some of Melinda's story from Kelly, Dolly became worried about the remarks Richard had made. Never in the accounts of Douglas' trial had anyone accused Charmain of abusing Melinda. Dolly knew who Charmain was from Richard's talking about his stepsister before. She hadn't been kind to him, either. He reported that on many occasions Charmain had deliberately broken toys and blamed it on him. Dolly suspected that it was with the encouragement or tacit consent of the stepmother at both the stepchildren had been mistreated.

Once summer vacation started, the school offered daily morning sessions of supervised play and crafts. Dolly was glad that the children had something to occupy their time. Donald was going to Boy Scout camp in August but Tinker, who said Boy Scouts was for sissies, wasn't interested. The social worker, Kelly, wanted Tinker to continue his weekly counseling sessions all summer as well. The sessions were held downtown in the Grant Building and had begun late in May. Kelly thought they were going well.

Until school was over, Dolly had picked him up on Wednesday after lunch and driven him to the sessions. It was going to be difficult to arrange this during the summer. Tinker himself came up with the suggestion that he go alone on the bus. The counselor had thought this was an encouraging sign and reluctantly Dolly had agreed.

Tinker was indeed glad for the freedom this provided. He wasn't at all pleased by the counseling sessions and hated the counselor, Dr. Kemp. During the sessions Tinker would draw pictures, which he considered "baby stuff" and then talk to the doctor about them. Most of the time he made things up but sometime he revealed the anger he felt at his mother for burning him with cigarettes when he'd been naughty. This would only intensify his anger. Anger that revealed that there was something he was trying to hide. Anger he wanted to fester and allow to grow.

Billy, Shirley and the rest of the children would go inside the school at ten-thirty to do craft work in the gym. They never seemed to miss Tinker. He enjoyed the morning playtime since he was a good basketball player and could push the other boys down while he hogged the ball and made baskets. When playtime was over, Tinker would wander off the playground and start casing the neighborhood.

The suburban houses were laid out on large lots. Most of

them were new, frame construction. A few, like the Erfer's were perhaps twenty years old and originally had been farm houses.

Living was casual. Bikes were left in yards and lawn furniture and picnic items were strewn in most backyards. On a good day, Tinker would find a back door open and a house empty. Then he would stroll through it at his leisure. Many times there was money tucked into drawers carelessly, which he didn't hesitate to appropriate. Now on Wednesdays when he was supposed to go from the school to the bus he found that he had plenty of spending money for candy and food.

Somehow, Tinker felt honor bound not to steal food but not bound by honor when it came to small items he liked in the department stores near the Grant Building. By the time he reached Dr. Kemp's office each week, his pockets would be bulging with his week's haul of gaudy trinkets he'd lifted from jewelry counters, toy departments and elsewhere. Although he'd always have a sick sensation before he started taking items, after the first one the thrill of accomplishment would spur him on to greater attempts. One week he stole an especially expensive pocket radio and he walked into the Grant Building puffed up with adrenaline.

Dr. Myron Kemp had been noticing an improvement in Tinker. Myron had gone to school at U.C.L.A. and felt he was doing his time in Dimsdale as a stepping stone up to a larger practice in Albany. He was thirty, short, skinny, balding, with close-set eyes that tended to glaze over when listening to a client. He always wore a suit even though it was summer and took pride in his well-blackened shoes and choice of ties. He felt it was necessary for his image. Most of his clients were referrals from the city welfare department but he was gradually building up a list of private patients.

His June report on Tinker spoke of him in glowing terms, enhancing his own image as a psychologist. He'd been unable to see that although Tinker was revealing a bit of his personal history that might explain his behavior, Tinker's anger was becoming intensified, not diminished.

On the day Tinker stole the radio, he entered the office with a grin from ear to ear.

"I'm glad to see you in such a fine mood," Dr. Kemp remarked.

Tinker winked. "Being able to come down on the bus by myself was a good idea. I'm having a fine time."

He didn't bother to elaborate with the fact that he'd had two and a half hours before the session to wander around, or what he held in his pocket. He kept his hand in his pocket, fingering the shiny case and the knobs on the side of it. He knew it wouldn't play without a battery. The battery he'd paid for. While the clerk was ringing it up he'd slipped the radio into his pocket, laughing to himself all the while. It was so easy.

"Would you like to talk or draw me a picture today?" Myron asked. "Did you ever think you might become an artist? You draw very well." One of his courses had been in interpreting children's drawings. He'd gotten an A and he felt he was adept at this kind of therapy.

"Naw, I'm going to collect garbage like my old man. Nobody likes to do it but us Italians, we kinda feel like it's a living," he said, repeating a phrase he'd heard his father make.

"You haven't talked about your father much before. He seems to have given you some advice. I thought he was living in Baltimore. When did you see him last?" Myron pursued this lead avidly since except on one occasion Tinker had avoided talking about his father.

"Must have been last Christmas, or the year before. He moved out about two years ago. Got a better job. Mom didn't mind much. He'd get drunk and bash her around a lot. Guess she deserved it." Tinker was suddenly aware that he'd revealed too much. His face flushed and he grabbed hard on the object in his pocket, reminding himself that he'd better start making up stories about what had happened for real before he was sent to the Erfers.

Saturday nights were vivid in Tinker's memory. Guido Marciano was born in Italy in 1921. He left a wife and three children to come help his elder brother who had started a prosperous private garbage hauling business. He'd promptly forgotten his Italian family.

Guido had a short temper, had an enormous build and although short, could lift things heavier than himself. But Tinker remembered his dad fondly. They had spent days fishing in the summer because Guido only worked nights. Tina, his mother, was red-haired, blue-eyed, tall and shapely. The parents were extreme opposites. She, too, had a quick temper and had never adjusted to motherhood. She'd resented Tinker from the time he'd been born. Tinker made it impossible for her to work at the bar where she'd met Guido one Saturday night. Caring for Tinker made her stay in the house when she would have been happier shopping for the gaudy clothing she loved. Tinker's arrival had also made her stingy.

When Guido would arrive home drunk on Saturday nights he would always be in the mood to go to bed with Tina. She would be in the mood for a fight, which eventually ensued. Not only had Guido spent most of the coming week's money but she was angry that she hadn't been able to go out. The brawl that ensued would be loud and violent. At times Guido would rip Tina's clothing in an effort to rape her. Tina tried all the kitchen implements in self-defense, pots, even knives.

Tinker would peek through the door of their bedroom until he couldn't stand the noise, for fear his father would

73

turn on him. Tinker would run out the house. In the nice weather he'd sleep in the backyard but when it got cold he'd have to huddle in a doorway down the street. By morning when he returned he'd find both of them asleep and when they woke, everything returned to normal. If normal was Tina's complaints about not enough money and Guido's complaints about not enough sex.

There were times when Guido didn't come home at all. This made it worse for Tinker. Tina would sit and brood and knit by the front window. Tinker could tell from the way she stabbed the needles in and out that her anger was getting hotter and hotter. No matter what he did she'd curse at him until finally she'd start beating him as if the disgust at her misery was centered on him. If he didn't cry enough she'd resort to burning him with her cigarettes. It seemed that she needed to include Tinker in her distress. His cries became the ones she wasn't able to utter.

For the remainder of the counseling session Tinker spun a web of creative lies in answer to Myron's inquiries. By the time he left after the hour of talking to the doctor, Tinker had wound himself into a tight ball. In effect, he'd trapped himself in his own web of lies and felt strangled and ready to explode. Myron seemed satisfied that most of the discourse had been believable. He couldn't wait to write down the part about how Tinker's mother had bought a piano and how his father smashed it.

Going home on the bus, Tinker chose a seat near the back. He usually sat next to someone who had a shopping bag that he could pilfer something from on the ride home. Today there was a young teenager dressed in shorts and a tank top in the second row of seats from the back. She smiled as he passed and he decided to pass up the opportunity for a chance of talking to someone nearly his own age. He started up a conversation which was one hundred percent bullshit about how his wealthy parents had sent him to the country for the summer and how he missed his "girl" back home.

By the time he got off the bus he'd gotten the girl's phone number and felt he'd made a conquest. When he entered the Erfer house it was quiet. There was a note on the bulletin board in the kitchen which said that everyone had gone for soft ice cream and that they'd be home soon. Tinker was relieved. Other weeks he'd had to wait for an opportunity to hide his loot when everyone was asleep. He'd been placing the stash in the closet in Melinda and Shirley's room inside the plastic bags that held the winter clothing. It took little to sort out some of the stuff. There were six lighters, lots of small cars, jewelry, perfume and scarves. Tinker wondered if the lighters still worked. Without taking it out of the bag he tried one of them. Instantly the bag caught on fire and ignited the clothing as well. Tinker ran from the room. He knew he should call the fire department but then everyone would know he'd set the fire so he ran out and down the street in the direction of the bus stop. He'd get on the bus and ride back toward town and come back later.

*   *   *

Dolly Erfer couldn't believe it when she turned onto the street. Two fire trucks were in front of their house and flames were shooting through the roof. She stopped the car in the middle of the block.

"You all stay in the car and don't leave for any reason," she shouted as she ran at breakneck speed toward the burning house. One of the firemen stepped in front of her as she rushed up the front walk.

"Lady, you can't go in there. I won't even let my firemen in there. That blaze is too hot!"

"But, it's my house. Everything I've got is inside!"

"Lady, I don't care. I can't let you in. Was there anyone in there? Did you leave your stove on or an iron plugged in? We might have been able to save more of it if we'd gotten the call immediately. We figure it was burning for at least ten minutes before we got the call."

"Thank God there wasn't anyone home. Unless Tinker was in there. I'd taken all the rest of the kids for ice cream but he was supposed to come home about now."

Dolly watched incredulously as the side wall collapsed, and then the roof. Lightning thoughts of what was inside and what she was going to do with her foster children crossed her mind. For the moment she was unaware that her family also would have to find housing and start from scratch.

She backed up, turned around, and slowly made her way back to the car, which she had forgotten to turn off. The children were gaping out the windows at the fire and black smoke which billowed upward. Shirley was crying. "My pretty pink bunny, where's he going to sleep tonight?"

Where were any of them going to sleep? Dolly tried to think. What should she do? Somehow the fire had mesmerized her and she sat in the car listening to the children's complaints and sobs with deaf ears. Her whole concentration was on what was happening to the house as it disintegrated into a pile of charred rubble. *How could it have happened? Where was Tinker? Was it possible that he'd set the fire?* Kelly had told her that he'd set some previously. Dolly didn't mention this to the fireman. At the time she'd been too stunned.

Although the fire was apparently out the men with the hoses kept pouring water on the mess that had been the home. "Look, here comes Tinker!" Billy said as he spotted him running from the direction of the bus stop.

"Gee, Mrs. Erfer, what happened? My bus was late

today and I saw the smoke from two blocks away. I never guessed it was our house. I'll bet Mr. Erfer will be plenty mad." Tinker poked his head in the car door.

"I'm just glad your bus was late," Dolly was roused from her lethargy. What would Chris say? That would be the first thing she had to do. Call him and tell him what had happened.

By now most of the neighbors who were home were out on their lawns looking at the fire. Two of them started walking toward the car. One of them offered to let Dolly use his telephone. Chris wasn't around the lumberyard when she called but one of the men said he'd round him up and send him home. At this remark Dolly started to cry. There wasn't any home left. The impact was gradually dawning on her and she knew that she had to call Kelly as it was past three o'clock and it would make it hard for Dolly to reach her since Kelly always made visits to clients in the afternoons.

Kelly Anderson was busy filling out reports at her desk when the call came. She'd never been able to accustom herself to the heat in upper New York State during the summers, since her home was in Canada. Her usual sloppy dress was augmented by a cotton scarf tied around her wispy hair Indian fashion. She hated this time of year when school was out and problems multiplied in ratio to the temperature.

She listened to the description of the tragedy with a skeptical awareness of Tinker's ability to falsify from past experience. She reassured Dolly that the Red Cross would take care of all of them for the time being until she could find other placements for the foster children. When she had made all the necessary arrangements she sat for a long time tapping her pencil on her desk. It wasn't going to be easy finding homes for all four children. Particularly Richard and Melinda, who seemed to need one another until they could rejoin their father. She doubted she could find another home in the middle of the summer that would take both children. Richard and Melinda wouldn't see one another for sixteen years, but no one knew this at the time.

7

Horse

The cell door came shut with a bang. Horse Pellam was livid. He hated his cell mate, Doug, and what had happened at the work shop had escalated the hate into a roiling boil. Horse was a fifty-five-year-old, burly, large-chested Irishman. He'd been sent to Tarrytown to do time for burglary and carrying a weapon. He was disgusted when he'd heard Doug was in for child neglect, even though Doug said it wasn't true. Horse had two kids, Ian and Mike, that were the joy of his life. He was sure that he'd never neglect them ever. After all, hadn't he been stealing for years to get them the best education and clothing?

How could the foreman in the shop have made Doug the supervisor of the lathes? Horse had been working in the shop for nine months, the longest of any of the prisoners, and figured that if anyone deserved being made supervisor it was himself. So what if Doug was an engineer? Seniority should mean something. Horse took a swing at the upper bunk with his closed fist. Even the hurt of his hand hitting metal didn't diminish the desire to do likewise to Doug's head when he came back from meeting with the foreman.

The last time Horse had lost his temper and taken a poke at Doug had been disastrous. Doug was nearly a foot taller than Horse and although he wasn't as heavy, he had had enough combat training in the Army to be able to defend himself well. Horse looked around the small cell for something with which to hit Doug that would make an impact. Every-thing was nailed down or bolted to the wall. Horse decided to wait and try to smuggle one of the heavy iron bars from the shop into the cell the following day.

All evening Horse didn't reply to Doug when he tried to have a conversation. Horse turned up his radio so loud that the guard had to come and tell him to cool it. At lights out, both men lay unsleeping in their bunks.

The following day was Saturday. Only a half a day in the shop because in the afternoons they allowed visitors to come. Horse waited for the guard to turn away so he could slip one of the bars he was tooling down his pant leg. He tried once and the guard came over and asked him what he was doing. From then on he felt the guard watching him more carefully so he went out of the shop with his plan postponed but far from forgotten.

The group of inmates who were expecting visitors were gathered after lunch around the side gate, where they could see a crowd already assembled. Horse expected Mike to arrive. He was going away to college in a few weeks and Horse knew that once he was in Pikeville, Kentucky, he'd not see him again until Christmas. He could see him waving to him before the gate opened.

Doug walked to the far end of the exercise yard, away from the groups of reunited families. He'd been expecting someone to come see him for the first few months, but although Dolores wrote, even she had never traveled the 120 miles to visit. As he turned away he saw coming toward him Esmirelda, who was waving excitedly. He'd never expected her to come since she'd not written or responded to any of his letters. Neither Sam or Charmain were behind her. As she neared, it appeared that she had either gained a lot of weight in the five months since he'd been away or that she was preg-nant.

"Hi, Douglas," Esmirelda threw her arms around Doug and tried to kiss him. In the intervening months Doug had had plenty of thinking time and come to the conclusion that the big reason he was behind bars was that Esmirelda had mistreated Melinda. He never could figure out why she hadn't shown up at the hearing or the trial, although his lawyer had tried to get her to come. The judge hadn't believed any of his testimony or Dolores' and neither had the jury.

Doug pushed Esmirelda back. "I didn't think you'd ever come see me. What do you want? Looks like you're pregnant again. Is that why you're here? Going to try to make me feel guilty like you did with Sam? You're the reason I'm here. I guess you deny that too."

Esmirelda rolled her big brown eyes in disbelief. She hadn't expected that Doug would be so bitter. Once he'd seen her with Sam this big he'd been proud that she was carrying his child.

"How can you blame me for what happened? I didn't know that Melinda was sick. I did think she was faking all those times she fell down and she wouldn't answer me. It wasn't until after the trial that I saw a program on television that explained about epilepsy. Now I understand. I've been so ashamed that I haven't come or answered your letters but I did think you'd like to know that we're going to have another baby in December."

It seemed impossible, but looking at Esmirelda's quivering lip, Doug felt the stirring of forgiveness. The thought of her guilt had been so firmly entrenched for so long that he didn't want to hear her explanation. He turned and started to walk away.

Es circled in front of him and put both hands on his arms and shook him. "Douglas, look at me. I do love you. I've come to tell you that I'm sorry and let you know what I've done."

"I know it will be hard for you to go back to Dimsdale when you get paroled. I think that will be sometime in the spring, so I've sold my house and moved to a farm outside of Ithaca. My sister and brother-in-law from Oklahoma are living in one of the houses on the farm and he's farming it for us. She's taking care of Sam and Charmain today. It will be much closer for me to come visit. That's one of the reasons I haven't come before, it was so far and I've been so sick for the first part of this pregnancy. I felt so responsible for your being in jail I thought you'd never forgive me."

"I can't be a farmer!" Doug was stunned by the adventurous streak that Es was displaying. "I'm not sure where I want to go when I get out, let alone whether I'll be coming back to live with you."

To himself he was thinking she might as well know that it wasn't going to be all that easy to have him forget and forgive what she'd done to not only his life but to the lives of Richard and Melinda. She hadn't mentioned anything about taking them back when he got out.

"Come on over and sit at one of the benches so we can talk," Es cajoled. "I want to tell you all about the farm. Of course you might not want to farm but it is close to both Ithaca and Syracuse where I'm sure you'd be able to get a job. Not only did I get a good price for the house, but Philomena, my sister, put up half the money for the farm. You might want to start your own business. By the time you get out the new baby will be about four months old and I remember how you enjoyed Sam when he was that age."

For over an hour, Es went on spinning her fantasy of how life for both of them would start anew. She described in detail the farm and the crops that they were planning in the spring. Potatoes and barley were planted, which Julius, her brother-in-law, had harvested at a good profit. There were two houses, a large barn and several outbuildings and some equipment that had come with the purchase. Doug was impressed at how little she had paid for all this.

Es described the house as a spacious two-story brick-and-frame dwelling and had brought some pictures of a charming neo-colonial which probably was eighty years old but in good shape. Douglas couldn't help but become intrigued and started asking questions about the heating system, roof and plumbing, as if he had a vested interest. He noted after a while that none of the future plans included Richard and Melinda.

As she'd been talking, Es had slid closer and closer to Doug on the bench and began first stroking his arm with her finger and then, not being rebuffed, started massaging his leg with her hand. Since there were many women in the groups nearby who were displaying even more aggressive behavior, not to mention some of the inmates who were rolling on the grass making out, Doug felt constrained to ignore the obvious attempts to revive his sexual feelings, particularly since Horse and his son were only twenty feet away and from time to time he'd seen Horse looking in their direction. Horse knew how Doug felt about Es and how he wanted to confront her with the fact that she should be the prisoner, not himself.

Now that she was here what would Horse think if he began to caress Es after all the despicable things he'd said about her? When Es reached over and grabbed his hand and put it on her bulging abdomen, Doug drew it away quickly. He knew she'd done this because she knew he'd always been intrigued by the feel of the motion of the baby when she was carrying Sam. He felt trapped. The urge to protect and comfort Es, particularly now that she was again carrying one of his children, was strong. The long-festering animosity kept getting in the way.

At the end of the hour, Es rose and once again attempted to put her arms around Douglas. Out of the corner of his eye he could see Horse saying good-bye to Mike. Doug wanted to return the embrace but kept his hands at his sides.

"I've a lot to think about. I do believe that you are sorry, Es. Come again in a week or so and maybe I'll have my feelings sorted out. Right now I'm ready to accept responsibility for this new child but don't count on too much more from me. In a way I'm sure I still have feelings for you but I've blamed you for so long I'll have to replay what you've told me before I can let you know what I'll do or where I'll go when my parole comes through."

Somehow Esmirelda had hoped for more than this. Her face screwed up into a frown and the unbidden tears started to roll down her face. "I've missed you so much. I do love you. I know this is difficult. Please forgive me. I'll be back soon." She grabbed his head with both her hands and brought it down so that she could kiss him on the lips. This was done so quickly Doug couldn't pull away and he felt her soft mouth, now salty from her tears, crushing against his. He responded automatically and then a rush of resentment swept through him and he pushed her away brusquely.

"It's not going to be that easy, Es. You were always adept at stirring me physically and if we weren't here I might take you to bed right now but that still wouldn't make things all right between us." Doug looked at the solemn face and hoped that Es was understanding his message. Her instincts had always been on a purely basic, sexual level. "You'd better go home and think things out. For one thing, you've never mentioned taking Richard and Melinda back and I'd want to know your intentions about them and answers to many other questions before I could make a decision on re-establishing a relationship."

"Well, good-bye then. And thanks for coming! If that's the way you feel I'll still be back in two weeks to see you," Es said sarcastically, abruptly turning her back. She moved swiftly toward the gate. Doug watched her swaying, enticing walk, which was slightly exaggerated by the displacement of her weight due to the baby. He heard one of the prisoners whistle and he knew that Es heard it too and knew it was for her for she turned her head slightly in the direction of the whistle and then tossed it suggestively, swinging her long black hair over her shoulder in the process. Just like a teenager, Doug thought.

*   *   *

"Looks like your honey brought you a present." Horse was feeling talkative again when he got back from saying good-bye to Mike. He'd been surprised to see Doug have a visitor and surmised that it was his wife. Since Doug, during the past few months, had told the story of Esmirelda, he wondered how Doug was taking the news that he was going to be a father.

"Yea, she's pregnant again. Must have been the last night before I was arrested. I'm having a hell of a time figuring her out. She claims she didn't know anything about Melinda being sick and that she wasn't to blame for neglecting Melinda, all of which I'm now being punished for. And to top that, she's sold her house and moved to a farm near here and wants me to come back and live with her. Just like that. Back into a strange community with a new family. Oh, yes, want to hear the kicker? Her sister and brother-in-law are living on the property too. And she didn't mention what would happen to my kids."

"Looks like you've got a few problems." Horse wasn't being sympathetic. He hid his resentment about Doug's job promotion but couldn't resist taking a dig at his cellmate.

"You're Catholic, aren't you? Seems to me it's your duty to go back to the woman and make the best of things. She isn't too bad lookin'. I will admit that. Walked like a floozy on her way out of the gate."

"But, I'm no farmer," Doug ignored the slur about Es's exit. "I thought I'd be able to set myself up in a business after a few years when I left here. I developed some new products for the engineering firm I worked for before I came here and I know that with the use of computers I could begin tooling metal to specifications that some of the companies we worked for would be capable of producing. She did say she had put some capital in the bank from the sale of her house."

Horse was quiet for a while. He began thinking over what Doug was faced with. Most of all he was interested in Doug's projected plans for a business of his own. It seemed that he did know a lot about the machine tool business. Maybe he deserved the promotion in the shop more than Horse had thought. For years, Horse had socked a lot of his loot away, thinking he'd go straight sometime or other. It was too soon to make an offer but it was worth thinking about. Maybe with Doug's know-how and Horse's capital, something could be worked out.

"You might as well face it, Doug, sooner or later that woman will get you to do what she wants. I know the kind. Super planners. You can't escape. You don't have to be a farmer. Be smart, let your brother-in-law take care of the farm. Get a job working until you can do what you want. Meantime you'll have the comfort of a family again. She's not all that bad, is she?"

"No, she isn't. Just naive and perhaps a bit stupid. It's ignoring the other kids, Richard and Melinda, that hurt. I want them to be part of my family too."

Both men were silent the rest of the evening. Horse didn't even brag about Mike and his conversation that afternoon. He'd made sure that Mike left with a good hefty wad of dough. Going to college meant everything to Horse. Mike and Ian were the first Pellhams in the family to get this far. Ian was in law school at Northwestern and Mike wanted to become a teacher. Trudy, Horse's wife, had been managing the investments that were kept in her name. They were showing a growing profit.

Douglas finally drifted off to sleep, trying to decide on some course of action which would make everyone happy. In his dreams he was overwhelmed with the sense of longing for someone to give him physical solace. He kept wandering through dark streets searching for someone who always seemed to be in the distance. After what seemed like an eternity he began to get closer to a form that began to take the shape of a female. Finally she turned and opened her arms. It was Rose who clutched him in her embrace and to whom he clung with intense desire.

Doug awoke, sweating and disoriented. The dream had been so real he had to focus on the blank wall and confined cell for several minutes before the realization of where he was dawned. He hadn't dreamed of Rose since Korea. Why had he dreamed of her now? He sat on the side of the bunk smoking a cigarette for a while, trying to shake the longing that filled his thoughts even though he was awake. Perhaps it was that not since Rose had he felt loved for himself alone. Was it possible that after so long he missed her so deeply that she was the only one he felt he could turn to?

It was hard to get back to sleep. Having Esmirelda show up had given him too many additional facets to cope with. He'd been thinking all along that when he got out, which hopefully would be shortly, if the parole board agreed to shorten his two-year sentence, he'd divorce Es and get Mom and Richard and Melinda back in a house. Like it was after he'd gotten back from the service. There were so many new complications. It was like working on a jigsaw puzzle for weeks and getting all but a few pieces done and having someone spill it and discovering there were dozens of new pieces that should fit in where there wasn't any room.

By morning, Doug had no solutions but was glad to return to the mind-blocking routine of the prison work detail. He wanted to try some of his ideas of increasing efficiency in the shop. He asked for time to talk to the foreman. To his surprise all his suggestions were met with interest. Some of them would require additional equipment and the foreman could see how they would expedite the milling of the work and allow for the bidding on more lucrative contracts. He promised to ask for an allotment of funds at the next board meeting.

Occasionally, when he passed Horse, he stopped to comment on how efficiently Horse handled the lathe. When he suggested that by moving the raw material to table height it would make the work go faster and require less bending, Horse immediately pushed a work table under the side of his machine and implemented the idea. As Doug walked around the room, Horse heard that he was making similar suggestions to others and he began to see that his anger at Doug's promotion was ill-founded. Doug was better than he'd ever be able to be.

As his anger at Doug began to cool down, he was faced with another problem. The bar he'd slipped into his shirt began to trouble Horse. He wouldn't have to use it after all, but now that he'd been able to secret it he'd better leave it there. Perhaps it wouldn't be missed in the count at the end of the shift. If he tried fishing it out he might be caught doing that and that would be even more difficult to explain.

With the changes that were occurring in procedure, the daily routine was moving much more smoothly and by three o'clock most of the men had finished their assigned work load. This made it necessary for the supply room to be re-opened and fortunately, the count was bungled by the foreman at the end of the shift. All of the men were praised for their increased production, due in part to their new supervisor, Doug.

Horse grudgingly acknowledged to Doug as they filed out, "My back doesn't ache like it generally does at the end of the day. Saving all that bending and lifting did help, and it was faster."

To himself he thought that investing some of his money on Doug's proposed computer tooling might be a good move after prison. He'd be getting out months before Doug, if the cards were right. Maybe he could scout around for a place to house a plant that Doug wanted. And to start ordering equipment that would make it productive. Doug did have a way of handling not only machines but people. Horse wasn't eager to spend his life behind a lathe but if he were part of management that would make it different.

Not for several weeks did Horse mention any of this to Doug. Monotony of routine work took both their minds off their personal problems. Es, true to her promise, did show up for another visit. When she did, Douglas talked again of his desire for having the whole family restored. He'd resigned himself to accepting the responsibility of the extended family. He even accepted the fact that he'd live on the farm, but try to find work elsewhere.

Es surprised him. She'd called Kelly Anderson in Dimsdale to inquire about the children. Doug was upset when he heard about the fire. He was even more distressed to learn that Richard and Melinda were now in separate foster homes. One of them was not even in Dimsdale. It had been impossible to find a placement for Melinda except in a nearby town. Esmirelda said Kelly had told her to call back when she was sure about when Douglas would be released.

What Es hadn't mentioned was that Kelly didn't think

that even though Doug and she were back together, the welfare association would approve the return of either of the children. Esmirelda had been insulted by the attitude of the agency toward her. Even over the phone she could hear the disdain Kelly displayed. She had tried to explain how she hadn't understood about Melinda's medical problems but Kelly kept asking probing questions concerning other things that showed she knew much more about what had happened than Es liked.

Secretly, Es hoped she wouldn't have to cope with Richard and certainly not with Melinda. Melinda probably would make Charmain seem stupid at school, like in Dimsdale. It would be ideal to start from scratch with only the new baby, Charmain, Sam, Doug and herself.

All Doug needed to know was that she had tried. He didn't need to know until later that it would probably be impossible to get his children back. Of course, once Doug heard that Es had been trying, he relaxed and agreed that this would be the best for everyone. His thoughts centered on counting the days until his release. Although he was enjoying improving the production facilities in the metal tooling room, he couldn't wait until he was released so that he could again plan for his dream plant.

After a while, even the weekly visits from Es began to be pleasant. Doug found that her early attempts to fondle him were welcome. He began cherishing the lingering kisses and remembering the good times in bed with Es. Soon after Thanksgiving, Es told him that she wouldn't be coming until after the baby arrived. The doctor didn't want her to be far away from home and the hospital. The weather had been worsening and Doug agreed that driving on slippery roads was endangering both the baby and Es. This meant that she wouldn't be able to come for any visits until after January.

Horse came back from his parole hearing jubilant.

They'd agreed to let him out December 2nd. Now was the time to broach the subject he'd been mulling over for weeks. He told Doug all about what he'd like to do when he got out. He'd already talked to his wife and she agreed that this was a wonderful opportunity. She'd checked on Doug's record at the plant in Dimsdale and came back with glowing reports. She'd also lined up some other investors who were looking for a place outside of Ithaca to establish a business. She'd even looked at houses for them to move to so that they could be nearby.

Doug was flabbergasted at the extent of Horse's interest and the amount of effort he had already put into the planning.

"Why didn't you tell me you were thinking about this? We could have been talking about this for weeks. I can't believe that you have enough confidence in me to go ahead with all this without knowing whether I'd even be interested. Don't get me wrong, I am. Extremely! I'm just amazed. Do you have any idea of the capital involved in such a project?

"I'd thought of starting with a small shop then introducing the computerized aspect later. The changes in the computer business may be extensive during the next ten years. I want to be in on the cutting edge. By the way, how much money did you have in mind investing? We're talking about big money."

"Several hundred thousand to start," Horse proudly explained. "If you need more I'm sure with that kind of security we could borrow it."

One thing Horse had learned, it wasn't necessary to steal money from banks. You could borrow it in someone else's name. Stealing jewelry and cash had proved to be lucrative, but the punishment too risky.

"How the hell did you get a hold of that kind of dough? When you said you were a burglar I thought you meant little stuff and that you'd had to return your loot."

Lies came easy to Horse. "My wife's an investment coun-selor. She's been very lucky in the market and has made many friends who like to share in a future profit-making opportu-nity."

This was partially true. The money he'd left in his wife's name had been invested well. What he didn't mention was that the source of half of the money came from the connec-tions his wife's family had with the Scambino family.

By the time Horse was released, the list of catalogs and contacts that Doug had given him filled six pages. Doug blindly believed the story and was so anxious to explore the possibilities of the project he'd been planning every since he'd worked on the big computer at Columbia. The possibilities when applied to advanced engineering were endless. That is why he'd made such good progress in the Dimsdale company and in the prison shop. He was creative. The plans for the coming plant of his own seemed too good to be true.

The replacement for Horse was a surly, skinny rapist who only spoke a few words of English. The language he spoke none of the inmates could understand, consequently he became a loner at once. Rapists were ignored, as a rule, so no one paid any attention to him anyway. His name too was dif-ficult. It was printed Bruzakowinsky. The guards and Doug called him Brew.

Doug wasn't unhappy that communication was limited. He had lots to think about. The baby arrived three days after Horse got out. It was a big, nine-pound, six-ounce boy that Es named Douglas, Jr. without even consulting Doug. The guard came and told him the news in the middle of a shift. Es's sister had phoned. Doug knew this was an exception to the rule but the foreman had let them know in the warden's office that Doug was doing an exceptional job. Because of this, Doug got special privileges. It was disheartening that he didn't get to see the baby immediately, but if there was no snow perhaps Es would venture the trip for Christmas after all.

Not only did Es bring the baby, but Sam and Charmain as well, two days before Christmas. Her sister, Philomena, had driven them in a borrowed station wagon. Doug was astonished at the difference in the two sisters. Philomena was tall and stately. She had the same dark hair and eyes but where Es's face was round and pudgy, her sister's was angular and with much paler skin. She looked like a *Vogue* model. Even her dress and walk were sophisticated. Where Es jiggled, Philomena glided. A very attractive woman.

Es's gift of a satin smoking jacket was not only inappropriate but impractical but Doug thanked her profusely and insisted that she take it home and keep it until his release. After she left, he chuckled at the thought of evenings he'd be coerced into wearing it. It was incredible how much both Sam and Charmain had grown. They hugged and kissed him and never mentioned the stark atmosphere in the crowded day room or the fact that he was in prison.

Only two more months. The thought kept ringing in Doug's head. The new calendar that Charmain had given him started to be filled with crosses as the end of January brought the hearing date for his parole closer and closer. Was it just a coincidence that it was set for Valentine's Day? If they approved it, it meant that he'd get out the first week in March. Only three weeks shy of a year since the end of his trial. It had been a long year but Doug had learned more management techniques dealing with the hard core men in the shop than he would probably need in the new plant.

The new plant! How incredible it sounded. Horse kept reporting on his success. By mid-January he'd found a small brick building that already had some metal working equipment. It was a tool-and-die works that had folded recently. Horse said the machinery was better than he'd worked on in prison. The price was good and they agreed to purchase it and the fourteen acres of woodland that adjoined the property. Horse had also found a house in Martinsburg that he would move into shortly. Doug was trusting Horse in all this.

Horse insisted that he buy a new truck for the plant and gave Doug the keys, "for safe keeping." When the hearing went well, Horse was the first person through the gate the next visiting day. "I'll be by to pick you up in your new truck!" Horse pounded Doug on the back and did a bit of an Irish Jig. "Just let me know the day you get out."

"That truck is for the company. By the way, what are we going to call it. We've been so busy talking about all the other plans I haven't given it much thought," Doug remarked.

"Thought Dixon and Pellham sounded just fine. Anyway, that's what's printed on the side of the truck. Change your mind and the new paint job's off your first week's salary. By the way, I hired a bookkeeper and a secretary last week. Of course you'll have to give the O.K. on both of them, but I couldn't wait. The plant is spic-and-span and ready to go. Do you want me to put an ad in the paper for some men?" Horse's enthusiasm spilled over into a rush of words.

"Hold on, you're going too fast. All of this doesn't have to be done immediately you know. I want to be there when we hire people. I want to build a force of workers that I know myself. As for the bookkeeper and secretary, I'm sorry you didn't wait but make sure that they will know they are on a trial basis. What in the world will you have them do in the next three weeks? What are you paying them? We haven't talked money at all. I don't even know how much you have left over after you bought the building."

Horse blinked. He'd never thought Doug might not be as excited about everything as he was, but after all, Doug was still in the can. Just wait until he got out. He'd change his tune. He didn't want to tell Doug that the bookkeeper was part of the deal he'd made in exchange for eight hundred thousand dollars. One of the "investors" wanted to keep an eye on the money.

"I thought we could both start out at twenty thousand and give ourselves raises as the business built up. That all right with you, Doug?"

"Mighty generous of you, Horse. Make sure you earn it," Doug scowled and furrowed his eyebrows. He had the first glimmer of not being in control of the operation. After all, since Horse was bringing all the capital he might think that he had equal say in the company. Doug wanted to keep control even at the expense of losing Horse's backing.

"For the record, I hope you realize that I intend to have full control over all the decision making in the company. I'll appreciate you taking over the responsibility of the day-to-day production but you'd better know from the start that since it's my idea, I'll have to make all the final decisions."

"Gee, Doug, don't jump to conclusions. You are in charge. I want to make everything as smooth as possible. Since I've been out and making all the arrangements I guess you thought that I was taking over. No, sir. You're the boss."

Horse reined in his enthusiasm. His tendency to want to take charge would have to be disguised as intense interest in the future. Horse was not a subtle man. He tended to call a spade a spade. Watching what he said had never been one of his strong points. Since he had already invested considerable time and money in the project he wasn't about to lose status at this juncture. On the surface from now on he'd have to make it seem as though he'd heeded Doug's warning.

The appearance of a truce on Horse's part didn't fool Douglas. After Horse had gone, Doug started to outline a strict line of command down to the last detail. He'd not show it to Horse but keep it for future reference. Horse might be supplying the money but the brains and creative ability were what would make it succeed. Judging from what he'd observed when he was working with Horse in the metal shop, he knew he could follow orders but only if given specific instructions. His creative ability hadn't surfaced when challenged with a new situation. It would be impossible to delegate any but the daily scheduling and maintenance duties to him. Doug didn't know how to implement the regulation and limitation of tasks to Horse without implying distrust of judgment. He hoped that he'd be able to work this out when the actual business started running.

The remaining weeks went by swiftly as he tried to train his replacement in the metal shop. True to his promise, Horse did show up when Doug was released in a huge red truck with the names Dixon and Pellham emblazoned in brilliant gold letters on the sides of the doors.

Horse was again enthusiastically outlining the progress he'd made in the intervening time. He'd had some of the land cleared and put in a large parking lot on the west side of the building. It was only gravel now but he said that in a few months he was going to have it surfaced permanently. He'd also arranged for a two-million dollar line of credit from a New York bank and was talking about a trip for them both to California to visit some plants where they were already using computer systems.

Most of this fell on deaf ears because Doug, who hadn't seen this part of the country, was staring out the window. Not only was it incredible that the prison was fading in the distance as the miles passed but that he wasn't going back to the home he'd left. All of this was so new he was thinking not about the industrial possibilities he faced but of the situation he probably would be faced with at home with Esmirelda and the extended family that awaited him. He found the prospects of seeing Philomena kept coming into his thoughts with pleasure. She'd seemed so friendly and beautiful he was looking forward to getting better acquainted. If only Melinda and

Richard would be waiting, things would be as nearly perfect as possible. *What had happened to Dolores?* he wondered. He hadn't seen her for nearly a year. At the first opportunity, he intended to visit her and try to bring her back to the farm for a visit.

Dolores had been faithful in writing Doug weekly but she hadn't told him any of the discomforting news about Harry. Early in the summer, Harry had been complaining about how often he had to get up during the night. When the doctor had examined him he found that he had not only an enlarged prostate but an operation had proved it cancerous. At his age they gave him estrogen therapy rather than a radical operation. However, he hadn't been driving for months, which was hard for both Tilly and Dolores. They had gone with some friends to spend three weeks at the lake in the fall.

This was one of the reasons she'd not been able to come visit Doug. For some reason, she'd not wanted Doug to worry about anything that was happening to her, so she concealed this news and invented an excuse for not visiting. Doug knew that it was a long trip and although he'd missed his mother he didn't question her absence or wonder why she'd spend three weeks at the lake and not try to come any farther.

"I want to see the new plant before you drive me home. Do you mind?" Doug brought himself back from his reverie about the homecoming and started to attend to Horse's description of the furnace he was thinking of installing.

"Sure thing. I thought you'd like to do that. Good thing that they left you out early. There'll be time to have a late lunch in town before we go. You'll like some of the restaurants in Ithaca. There's a real nice one downtown. I want to treat you to a fine meal. Nothing like that slop they gave us in the can. What have you been hankering for? I know, a good, thick, juicy steak and all the trimmings, right?"

Food was the last thing on Doug's mind. He'd never been

one to savor food or have gourmet desires. The Army and prison had food that was mediocre but nourishing. Neither his mother or Es had been exceptional cooks. One meal was more or less the same to him.

"Thanks, but no thanks. Let's stop at a diner or something. That will be fine. You can treat both Es and me to dinner some other time."

It was disappointing to Horse because he was accustomed to taking lunch out in a good restaurant but he imagined Doug was anxious to get on to see the building he'd purchased, so he turned off at the next intersection of the highway and took a shortcut which would put them within a few miles of the new plant.

They passed through a small town which was no bigger than a few houses, and a country store on the main street. There was a small diner on the edge of town which, at two in the afternoon, had only one customer. The hamburger was large and the service pleasant. Doug changed his mind and included a remarkably good home-baked cherry pie with ice cream in his order. Refreshed and full they drove for another twenty minutes along gravel-paved roads that were lined with what promised to be a canopied bower of willow wands that already had their first wisps of yellow on their tips.

"You can see it from here. Just past that rise you can see the smoke stack and the top of the building. Look, Doug, this is all ours. Lock, stock and barrel."

The low-lying plant was a few hundred yards from the shore of Lake Cayuga and, as Horse had mentioned, along the west side was a large parking lot. As they drew closer, Doug couldn't help but be impressed with the size of the building.

Once they were inside the building the space seemed to go on and on. There was much more space than Doug had anticipated from the photos that Horse had brought him.

More space than they would need in many years at the rate of production he'd anticipated. It was probably hard to heat as well, with no divisions to prevent heat from filling the entire space.

"Hi, Mr. Dixon. I'm Joan Winston, your secretary." A small-framed young woman with startling blue eyes and mousy brown hair fixed in a bun came out of the office door near the entrance. Douglas was startled at seeing her coming toward him with an outstretched hand.

"I didn't see any cars in the parking lot. I didn't think anyone was here. I'm pleased to meet you. Please show me what kind of office space we have here and what equipment we have. Since you're already working we might as well start by having you take the notes as I go around inspecting the property."

"My husband drops me off on his way to school every day and picks me up in the evening. That's why you didn't see a car. Come on in and let me show you your new office. Mr. Pellham and I have tried to think about everything you might need and I think you'll like it." Joan went past a row of outer desks and opened a door at the rear of the front office and beckoned Doug to follow.

The room Doug entered was about twenty feet square and had one outside window which faced the parking lot. The walls were lined halfway up with oak paneling and the upper walls covered with a pale shade of tan. Several well-done water colors of local scenes in large frames were evidence of someone's good taste. A large mahogany desk faced the window and three comfortable chairs were placed nearby. In one corner a plant stand held a philodendron of massive proportions. Obvious care had been taken to supply good technical books in the bookcase opposite the door. The list he'd given Horse had been more than adequately filled.

Doug couldn't resist the impulse to walk behind the desk

and sit in the imposing black leather chair. He noted the intercom and telephone system were multiple choices of communications and the huge computer took up one whole side of the room.

"Someone has been following suggestions very well. Is it you, Joan? I'll need a two drawer file cabinet. Put it in the outer office. Get me a log book and a supply of drafting pens, a large memo pad, some cards for the computer and a printer."

As he dictated these items, Doug was busy pulling out drawers and noting that already someone who was familiar with office procedures had outfitted the desk with most of the necessary items he'd require. Joan was busy taking notes as he spoke. She smiled at the reference of carrying out requests. Each time Horse had come back from visiting Doug, she'd made sure he handed her the new list of items to be taken into consideration. Her three years in the bursar's office at Cornell had come to good use. She had never been told that Doug was in prison but that he was at some distant spot planning all this.

"Let's go look at the machinery and the rest of the building."

Doug rose and started striding out of the door at a brisk pace. Getting used to this was going to be easier than he'd thought. As he examined the existing machines he began to doubt Horse's ability to evaluate anything except on a superficial level. Although Horse had told him the kinds of machines there were already in the building, he'd not been conversant enough to note that for the most part the machines were antiquated and in some instances rusted beyond refurbishing.

Another concern was the low overhead space, which wouldn't allow any crane activity for moving heavy metal from place to place. The wiring was inadequate for the kinds of loads the machines would need if everything was going at full capacity. The employees washrooms, something until now he'd neglected to consider, were in disastrous condition, as was their lunchroom and locker area.

One by one the discouraging discrepancies between Horse's descriptions and reality became alarmingly apparent. Gradually over the period of the next half hour, Doug's anger rose. Except for the areas where the employees were concerned, he'd not mentioned any of the mounting problems. It would do no good to confront Horse in front of his new employee. Some of the things that needed correction could be taken care of, but they would have to start from scratch and order almost all new machinery before anyone could conceive of going into production. This would mean the expenditure of hundreds of thousands of dollars.

Perhaps it would be best to have it out on the way to the farm in the truck. It might be better to start from scratch and buy a new building than to try to correct everything that was wrong. The chilly air as they left the building helped clear Doug's head. Before he had a chance to broach the subject Horse inquired.

"You were mighty quiet in there. What did you think of the place? That office set us back plenty but it was worth every penny to see your face when you settled into that desk chair and started rummaging through that desk. And how do you like Mrs. Winston? Super efficient, I can tell you. She thought of everything. Even those pictures."

"Horse, I don't know where to begin. There are a lot of things wrong with the building and the machinery. I'll try to explain. I'm not blaming you. You did the best you knew how but I have to tell you that almost none of the present machinery will do. Also, the ceilings are too low to install proper cranes to move heavy stuff. The heating bill is going to be astronomical unless we build a temporary wall and re-do the ducts. We'll not be able to use all that space for many years.

All of this is going to cost a lot of money. Maybe we should try looking at another building that is smaller and more modern. That's another thing, the place will need new wiring soon. Another big expense."

For some while Doug thought perhaps Horse hadn't heard or understood what he was talking about because there was complete silence. Expecting to see Horse's lantern jaw working furiously as it did when he was angry, Doug turned in his seat. Instead Horse's head had dropped down on his chest and he was moving his hands up and down on the steering wheel rhythmically.

All the excitement and enthusiasm of the past three months seemed to be coming out the ends of his fingers. The place they were coming from was the pit of his stomach, which now held a large black empty space that kept growing with each deep breath he took. Horse surmised in his misery that the decisions over these months that he'd made in haste were falling down around his ears. He'd felt like this before. Each time one of his burglaries had been thwarted by the police. The same sensation of exhilaration that had proceeded the job had been replaced by the devastating feeling that once again he hadn't been as smart as he'd thought. All the elaborate plans had come to naught. *Was it too late to salvage something? He'd meant this to be a way to go straight at last. Had he botched this too?*

"Did you hear me?" Doug shook Horse's arm. "What are we going to do? This was, and is, a good idea. How are we going to solve these problems?"

"Hell, man! I'm trying to think. What you said blasted all my guts that I've put into this to pieces. I don't know what to do. I do know that there are darn few places in this area that have even that much space. I've looked. As for the money, there's plenty more where that came from. I don't want to look like a darn fool in front of Trudy's uncles and tell

102

them that all the money I've spent so far is down the tubes."

Now it was Douglas's turn to be quiet. Finally he said, "We'd better explore the cost of getting new machines and get an engineer in to see if he could rig something to move heavy metal around without an overhead crane. Then a contractor to give us some bids on closing off part of the plant. After that we can come to some decisions."

"That's why I latched on to you. I knew you were smarter than me." Horse begrudgingly acknowledged his shortsightedness. "When you come in tomorrow we'll start working on all those angles right away. It's a good thing I hired Joan. We'll find lots for her to do."

They had been driving along in the direction that they had come for several miles. Doug had been so busy talking he'd not noted that they now were off the road and onto a dirt lane which led through open field. In the distance he could see some trees and a few buildings and barns. As they got closer, he spotted Sam running around inside a fence chasing a chicken.

"Is this where Es lives? Is all this land ours?"

"Sure is. That wife of yours got a bargain when she bought this place. There is one more surprise for you and I hope this one doesn't backfire. I've left you a present in the barn. It didn't come out of the company money. It's a gift from me to you. Kinda a thank-you for having the idea that is going to change our lives." Horse pulled the truck up beside a tin-sided barn and was pointing inside.

The double-hung barn door was open and in the dim interior, Doug could see the outline of a car. He hopped out of the truck and walked into the barn. A brand-new dark-green Volkswagon bus greeted his amazed stare. He turned and took a swing at Horse's arm with his fist. This was as close to an embrace he could muster.

"You son of a gun! You didn't have to do that for me. I

don't know what to say. I've never had a new car in my life."

Horse looked sheepishly in the direction of the floor. "Couldn't have you showing up for work late. Besides, you're an executive of a going business. You've got to look the part."

Charmain and Es crowded into the barn. When they'd seen the truck come up the road they'd come hurrying out to greet them. Doug looked beyond them, expecting to see Richard and Melinda. "Where is everybody else?"

"Philomena is in town and the baby's asleep. I think you saw Sam when you drove up. Bill is probably taking care of some farm chore. I never know what he's up to. He's always going, never stops, busy, busy, busy."

"Where are Melinda and Richard? I thought they'd be here."

Es didn't answer the question and was hurrying across the farmyard and into the house, calling over her shoulder. "Come on inside. I want you to see what we've done with the house. We just finished painting the bedrooms."

"I'm not coming in. Got to get back home to Trudy and tell her all about everything. See you tomorrow at eight?" Horse was already back in the truck cab.

"I'm not following the prison schedule anymore. At least the first morning I'm home, I don't intend to bust my butt in getting up at six. See you nearer nine-thirty. Business hours, you know. By the way, I wasn't paying too much attention on the ride over. How do I get there?"

8

Virginia

It had seemed a long eight months but things were beginning to hum at Dixon and Pellham. Most of the machines were working efficiently and recruiting for technical help had brought men from as far away as Massachusetts. Walking through the plant on his daily inspection tour Doug was pleased with the first production outlook. He'd never doubted the market for his invention. Once companies knew that with his computer-enhanced programs he could supply them with parts in half the time he'd had a client list that was growing daily.

After a lot of expensive adjustments they had stayed in the original building. The work force numbered thirty-seven, including four in the office. There was already talk of expanding into the section that had been concrete-blocked off to conserve heat. What pleased Doug most was the fact that the worries he had about Horse were proving unfounded.

The scare that his initial planning had backfired had made Horse cautious in suggesting any radical changes. He was content to carry out the orders Doug gave him and to run all the paper work to and from the bank. He'd not protested when Doug hired a fireman, the job Horse thought he was going to have. The business was going to show a profit in a few years and that was certain.

One thing troubled Doug from time to time. The welfare agency had still not given approval for Richard and Melinda to be returned to him. His lawyer, Horse's son Ian, had asked for a custody hearing which had turned out badly. Kelly Anderson had proved that Esmirelda had made no contact with the children while they were in placement. The judge, after reading the transcript of Doug's trial, had maintained that unless he was able to prove that they would not again be mistreated, he couldn't give Doug custody since it was his opinion that Es had contributed to the neglect.

He had taken one weekend to visit both children and Dolores. The home where Richard stayed had two other foster children and was in the center of Dimsdale. Richard seemed only mildly interested in seeing Doug. He kept calling Toby Lear, his foster parent, Ma. He ran off to play with the other children after saying, "Hello" and answering a few questions. Toby, a rotund thirtyish blonde woman with buck teeth, told Doug that Richard was adjusting nicely. She'd been worried when he first arrived because of the separation from Melinda. After a few months, he'd stopped talking about her completely.

Melinda's foster home was eight miles south of Dimsdale. Kelly had explained how difficult it was to place a child with medical problems. Dimsdale frequently placed children in other homes in the county. The town was still responsible for payment but since Dimsdale gave more per day than other communities it wasn't hard to find placement in the outlying towns.

Douglas saw before he'd entered the house that Maude Scoville's home was very different from the one where Richard was. The yard in late summer appeared to have been mowed only once, weeks ago. Broken bikes and toys lay pell mell on the walk and in the tall grass. It was doubtful that the house had seen paint for years. As he waited for someone to answer the bell, he could hear screams coming from the back of the house.

Just as he prepared to circle the house to see if there was an emergency, the door popped open and a small face appeared, looking through the screen door. Inside a child of about three, completely naked, stood staring at him.

"Is Melinda here?" Doug asked. He could see into the room and hear the television blaring. A group of children were sprawled on the floor with their backs to the door. The child pushed open the screen door and motioned for Doug to enter.

"Hey, anybody...Is Melinda here?" Doug shouted above the sound of the television. One of the children stirred, then seeing Doug, jumped to her feet and ran to him and hugged him hard around the knees.

"Daddy, Daddy, I didn't know you were coming. I'm so glad to see you. Are you going to take me home? I miss you so much. And Richard too. Is he outside in the car?"

It was hard to believe that the girl clinging to him was Melinda. Her beautiful blonde curly hair had been cut so short and was so dirty it gave her an elfin appearance. She had grown much taller. Her clothing was a sleeveless man's tee shirt that hung down to her knees. She had no shoes on and hadn't been bathed recently. Melinda's arms and legs were thin and scabs were on both knees.

"Where's Mrs. Scoville?" Doug could still hear the loud screaming coming from the rear of the house. He assumed that some emergency was engaging her attention. "I want to ask her if I could take you out to lunch. Be a good girl and go and get washed up and dressed while I talk to her."

"She's out back walloping Leon. He stole some bread and she's giving him what for. I'm sorry, I can't get dressed unless she tells me to. I only have one dress that I wear when Miss Kelly comes. She lets all of us dress up then. I would love to go to lunch though."

Maude Scoville appeared in the doorway as Melinda finished this revealing statement. She was dressed in a grimy sundress which allowed most of her ample torso to ripple over the top. Like the children, her feet were bare. She seemed to be about fifty but might have been younger. Her rotund face was wrinkled as though in a permanent frown. Her uncombed hair stuck out at odd angles around her face. Looking at her, Douglas vividly remembered old movies with Tug Boat Annie. This woman had a resemblance but with no smile. In fact her first words made him sure that smiling was not part of her repertoire.

"What cha doin' here, mister? I don let anyun tu come inter da house les I say so. Which one of you good fer nothin's let this guy in? I'll give you what fer! As fer you Linda, don be tattlin' bout our bisnes. Git upstairs I'll git rid of dis guy and while yer thar make sure yer room's tidy."

"I'm Melinda's father. I've come to ask you if I could take her out for lunch. I haven't seen her for some time and would like to spend several hours with her. I had suggested that she go upstairs and wash and get dressed but if you object I'll take her the way she is."

"Miss Kelly didn' tell me yud be comin. She knows I can't let a kid go with no say so from her. Git outa here."

"Maybe this note will explain. I'm only in town for the weekend and there wasn't time for her to call you before she left the office on Friday. If you read this note I'm sure it will be all right."

Maude reluctantly grabbed the paper and studied it with a squint. It seemed that either she had difficulty seeing without glasses or couldn't read at all. She shoved the note back at Doug and grunted.

"Well, I 'pose it'll be O.K. but make sur ya git back 'fore six." Maude moved to the stairs and bellowed to Melinda to get dressed. "Set yurselve down. No better wait in da car."

Sitting at lunch in a small restaurant in town, Doug was

amazed at the quantity of food Melinda consumed. After wolfing down a burger and fries she asked for another and a repeat of the chocolate milkshake. To top this off she consumed a large banana split. In between stuffing her mouth Melinda kept up a barrage of questions about the family and information about her foster home.

She said there were seven foster children living at the Scoville house. They were mostly from one to four years old. Melinda was the oldest and expected to care for the younger ones. She said she liked the babies and was good at changing diapers. There was no Mister Scoville that she knew of but Maude did have a man who came to visit overnight sometimes. Melinda's descriptions of the miserable food, cruelty and lack of cleanliness left Doug with the impression that except for the money, Maude wasn't interested in the children at all.

The temptation of taking Melinda immediately to his mother's was surfacing the longer Doug listened. He knew that since it was the weekend he couldn't get in touch with Kelly Anderson at the agency, but he was reluctant to have to take his daughter back to a miserable situation. However, Doug didn't want to have any more complaints lodged against him because it would be more difficult to obtain custody in the future.

He settled for taking Melinda on a shopping binge back in Dimsdale. Since school would be starting shortly, he purchased school clothing and shoes.

Then he took her to a toy store and let her pick out some toys and a doll. She asked him to keep the doll for her for when she could come live with him. The tears were hard to hold back when Melinda said this. As they were leaving the store, Melinda spotted a scarf on one of the counters and stopped to admire the soft silk and pretty colors. On impulse Doug purchased it and immediately she tied it around her head, disguising her mangled hair.

They stopped at Tilly's house for an hour and Melinda sat in Dolores' lap while they told one another how much each had missed the other. Then Melinda proudly displayed her new clothing. When she removed the scarf to show it to her grandmother, Dolores was appalled at the condition of the child's hair and immediately took her upstairs and gave her a shampoo. When they returned, the short hair was in ringlets and looked charming.

"Time to leave," Doug soon announced. On the way back to Maude's they stopped again for something to eat. This time Melinda ate more slowly and relished each bite. Doug promised that he'd make sure she didn't have to be at Maude's for much longer. To himself he promised that if she wasn't moved shortly he'd kidnap her and keep her until another placement was found. When they arrived at the Scoville house, Melinda rushed into the house dragging most of the packages. Doug followed with the remainder.

Maude stood in the center of the living room brandishing a stick. "You kids better sit and not budge 'til I sen' ya up ta bed," she admonished the cowering little ones who were sitting on the floor in front of the television.

She turned when they entered and grabbed the packages from Melinda. "What's dis? somethin' fer me?" Her greedy expression made Doug aware that he'd made a mistake in not thinking of including something for her on the shopping trip.

"I bought Melinda some school clothing and a few toys that she might want to let the other children play with. It was foolish not to have brought you back something too. Let me give you a few dollars for all your trouble with Melinda." This latter was said tongue in cheek. Doug reached into his wallet and handed Maude two ten-dollar bills. At this she was mollified and grinned and promptly placed them within her ample cleavage.

"Hope ya ate, cause we did." It was obvious when telling Doug to return by six Maude had intended that Melinda go without dinner.

"We did stop and eat a little while ago but I'm sure Melinda would like a snack before she goes to bed."

"No snacks after dinner. That's my rule." Maude frowned at the suggestion. She eyed this father with suspicion. She noted that Melinda's hair had been shampooed. This father wasn't like most of the other kids' folks. He was sharply dressed and knew how to get around. She became wary. Turning to Melinda she asked in as sweet a tone as she could muster, "What's in da bags? Show me yur stuff."

From the first bag, Melinda pulled a soft brown teddy bear. This she handed to one of the little boys. She continued to pull out toys and hand them to the other children. Doug realized that although she hadn't mentioned it while they were shopping, she'd intended to share the toys with her fellow foster family later. Once again, he felt tears close to spilling over and had to turn his head. By now all the children were excitedly enjoying their new toys and talking and playing gleefully.

Without warning, Maude picked up her weapon and swung it around the playing children, hitting several in the process. She snatched the toys from them and piled them up on the couch. "Wad I tol ya? Up to bed, all of yu, Melinda too. I'll let ya play wit dem toys when I'm good and redy."

The children, now frightened, without delay marched up the steps silently. This was a display of intimidation Doug had witnessed on occasion while he was in prison. He shuddered at the thought that Maude was like a jailer, with no love or understanding of the needs of the children she was keeping under her stringent rule. When he talked to Kelly he'd try to make her understand that not only Melinda but all of the children deserved better.

111

Melinda was the last to go and although she wanted to turn and say good-bye to Doug she knew that Maude wasn't to be angered further. Her good intentions of bringing the toys had come awry. She doubted that the children would ever see the toys again. They'd disappear like all the other gifts that were brought for them. She had managed to grab the bags which held her new clothing and take them with her.

Doug called to her as she went, "Remember my promise. I hope I'll see you soon." To let her know that he understood about what had happened with the toys he added, "I'll keep your doll safe for you."

After numerous phone calls the following week, Kelly let him know that Melinda was in another home. Her attempts to find a suitable placement once again were hampered by the fact that it was summer and that Melinda had a special medical problem. This was a pattern that neither Kelly or Doug suspected would be repeated almost yearly for the next seven years. Doug tried to arrange that Melinda come to the farm for the Christmas holidays. He was dismayed when Kelly called late in October to say that Melinda had related her experience with the doll a few Christmases ago to her and that the agency couldn't risk having her go back as long as he was still living with Esmirelda. Richard said he wanted to stay with his foster family for Christmas. So neither child would spend Christmas with him.

Douglas was disappointed but felt helpless. He found that Es was being a good mother to Sam, Charmain and Douglas Jr. His relations with Es were neither good or bad. They had gotten into the pattern of going their own separate ways. He was busy with the business. Es with the house and children. In bed, Es managed to tease him into lovemaking occasionally. It was as if a truce had been made. Douglas felt he couldn't desert these younger children for the sake of Richard and Melinda. Gradually over the period of many months he put both the older children in the back of his mind.

There was plenty to keep him occupied at work. Although the amount of business kept growing, there seemed to be a difficult time getting ahead financially. Virginia Burger, the bookkeeper Horse had hired, appeared to be doing an adequate job. However, when she was asked to produce a balance sheet, it indicated that there was a deficit. She always had a logical explanation and would point out all the expensive items that Doug was purchasing.

Virginia resented having to pull up roots from her comfortable job in Buffalo to go to this fledgling company that was being financed by Horse's wife, Trudy's, uncles. At sixty she had been looking forward to retirement in the job she'd overseen for a long time. It involved keeping watch over the laundries and restaurants in Buffalo where there was money to be laundered and sent out of the country. When Tony Albens had told her that it was a special favor to the "Boss," Virginia knew that this meant it was a direct order and that she dare not argue. Her additional instructions weren't hard to understand. She was quite accustomed to making business show a loss so that more money could be removed and the obligations to the borrowers reinforced by bigger and bigger debt.

This has been easy in Buffalo since most of the owners had little or no knowledge of books and finance. It was becoming harder and harder to fool Doug. He asked too many questions and was beginning to ask for invoices to back up purchases. She would have to become more adept. Since there were new employees being hired frequently it wouldn't be hard to fake an employee's records. The profit that was in actuality being made was being skimmed back to the organization.

Joan Winston, Doug's secretary, had tried to make

friends with Virginia during the weeks when there was little to do in the office. Virginia knew that this was one of the rules of "the Boss." No fraternization made life lonely but it was safe. There was never a possibility of a slip being made that would indicate that there was a hidden reason for her having the job. Virginia was single, by choice, and had become slovenly in her appearance. She came to work wearing mismatched clothing, runs in her stocking and unwashed hair. This made her appear frumpy and had it not been for her seeming mastery of the accounting procedures Doug would have thought of replacing her.

"I don't understand it," Doug complained to Horse at the end of the first year. "We've been getting more and more orders and cutting the time on each order shorter and shorter. Where am I going wrong? I think we should be showing a profit by now. Do you think we should hire someone to do an efficiency study?"

"Businesses aren't to show a profit the first year. At least that's what Trudy's uncle told me. Some of them take three to five years. You have to remember we spent a lot getting everything set up. Besides those loans had a high rate of interest."

Doug continued, "I'm sure Virginia is doing her job well, but I'm wondering about some of those items on her last balance sheet. Would you go over it with me?"

He wanted to share the responsibilities with Horse as much as possible. Horse probably wouldn't understand the complex figures but he wanted to reassure Horse that he was included in decisions since Horse was the one who had bankrolled it.

Horse pretended to concentrate on the sheets Doug placed in front of him. He shuffled them back and forth for a few minutes and mumbled something to the effect that it appeared O.K. to him. On his way out of the office he stopped at Virginia's desk and Doug noticed him having a serious conversation with her.

Doug would have been surprised to hear Horse say, "You'd better watch what you're doing. He's talking efficiency expert. If one of them get on to what's happening, we're in dutch. Don't worry, I know what's happening. Trudy told me. Her uncle needs this business so that he can disguise where his money really comes from." Horse also was being told just enough to keep him from being too curious.

That evening Virginia placed a long distance call to Tony Albens in Buffalo. "I'm in over my head with this job at Horse's. I've used all the tricks I know to make this business look like it is losing money so that we can continue to borrow more and more from you. Doug is clever. This business he's got going is taking off like gangbusters. He seems to be on the edge of a market that will only get bigger and bigger and show more and more profit."

"How about if I arrange to have him start another branch on the west coast? That would take a lot of additional capital and keep him out of your hair," Tony suggested.

"Just how are you going to do that? It seems like a good idea and it would take a lot of doing." Virginia seemed doubtful that Tony could swing something that big. He wasn't that high up in the organization for him to be suggesting anything that complicated.

"Don't worry. Trudy told me you might be having trouble and I asked around. Seems like the boss has connections in Washington State that are interested in the computer business. It must be a coming thing. Anyway, leave it to me. In a few weeks Doug will get an offer that is too good to refuse."

True to his prediction, Tony arranged that a call come in the following spring from an airplane manufacturer on the coast asking Douglas to come as a consultant in converting their assembly line using computer technology.

115

For a month Doug tried commuting back and forth but as the work became more involved he found that his experience was necessary on a daily basis. There were so many different processes involved in the manufacture of large airplanes he was kept busy many evenings and weekends as well. He finally rented a small house near the plant. When Es complained and wanted to move out too, he persuaded her to stay in New York, for the children's school would be starting soon. In fact, he was finding being without Es was a relief and his bachelor existence suited his lifestyle.

To Doug's amazement, when he was nearing the end of his contract, a plant in California who had heard of his abilities asked him to undertake similar computer-enhanced drafting for them. Doug hadn't been home except for Christmas and he felt he had to check on the New York plant, so before assuming the California job he went back to check the progress. The monthly reports had been encouraging under the supervision of the manager he had promoted from the staff there. Knowing that this couldn't have been accomplished without proper supervision, Doug needed to assess the progress himself.

Virginia was sitting at the outer office desk when he arrived with a girl on each side of her going over some ledger sheets. Neither one of the girls were familiar to Doug and since he'd not been informed of their hiring, he immediately interrupted and asked who they were and why he'd not been informed. Virginia smoothed his feathers and explained that they'd just been hired to help her with the expanding payroll and to do an inventory. Doug grabbed the ledger sheets and took them with him into his inner office.

Virginia winked at Dawn and Teal, the new girls. Tony had sent them when she had phoned for help. "I'm sure he won't spot the discrepancies. You girls are a big help with your new ideas of hiding what we are doing." All of them settled down at their desks. Smugly, Dawn took out her nail file and sat doing her nails.

Everything demanded Doug's attention. After being away for almost a year he found it was almost like a strange business as he walked through the plant. There were many new employees, all of whom seemed to be efficient. The foreman had hired an assistant and convinced him in a brief period of time that there was a great need for an addition to be put on the side of the plant to increase production and keep up with the flow of new orders they were getting. Doug hadn't thought they would get to this stage for several more years.

Stanley Sims, the foreman, obviously was a capable employee. In his spare time he'd gone to Cornell to take some computer courses so that he now was able to implement the instructions that came from the office with greater knowledge and efficiency with such confidence that Doug was impressed. Stanley suggested they conference with an architect he recommended who not only could plan the new addition but had enough knowledge of machinery to help with the technical design as well.

By the time Doug went home that evening he was convinced the plant was running well and that his original plans were being carried out more than satisfactorily. The only thing that puzzled him was despite the progress, his balance sheets weren't showing the profit he'd hoped for. Of course, the new addition would mean having to borrow more money. He wasn't concerned about getting it this time. Any bank looking at the progress would be happy to give him a loan. When he mentioned this to Horse the next day, Horse protested, saying that he was sure that Trudy's uncle would be happy to once again provide the capital.

Since the time in New York was brief, Doug gave in and asked Horse to arrange the financing rather than wait to have the bank approve a loan. At home, Es and the children, though glad to see him, seemed also to be getting along well without him. Es welcomed him back in bed but seemed content to see him go back to California at the end of the week. Time was too short to go see Melinda or Richard but he did talk to their new social worker about planning a summer visit in California.

One consultant job led to another for the next several years and except for occasional trips back home Doug was on the road all over the United States and occasionally in Europe. The field of computers was becoming more sophisticated as they managed to get smaller and more portable. His systems also were becoming more in demand.

After a while, Richard, Melinda and the rest of the family were seldom on his mind. One weekend while having a brief respite in Palm Springs at a company president's home, Douglas met Connie Feil. She was a thirtyish stylish blonde who was beginning a career using her well-developed skills in computer programming. Douglas was impressed with her and immediately offered to hire her as his assistant. He was beginning to feel the necessity for having a regional office on the west coast. After she accepted they found that the alliance worked well not only in the office but in bed, too.

9

Dolly

On the bed lay the neatly folded black cap and gown, awaiting Melinda's graduation. As she gazed in the mirror, Melinda felt sad since she knew she'd soon be eighteen and no longer the responsibility of Dolly Erfer. It had seemed a miracle when four years before, Melinda had once again been placed in Dolly's care. Melinda was sure she'd not be the valedictorian at her graduation if she'd stayed in one of the other miserable foster homes she'd been forced to endure since the fire had destroyed Dolly's home, years before.

Now she was the only foster child and Dolly's sons were away in college. Melinda had this cheerful room for herself. Dolly was now widowed and tried all the resources she knew to get Melinda a college scholarship, to no avail. Even though she had assured Melinda she could stay past her eighteenth birthday, Melinda knew Dolly wouldn't be able to afford to keep her without the extra money the county contributed for her care.

All along Dolly had used part of the money to pay for singing lessons, pretty clothes and other kinds of things teenagers wanted. Melinda called Dolly "Mom," and was extremely fond of her. In fact, no one at school knew that she wasn't her real mom. Melinda had only dim memories of Rose. She'd never considered Esmirelda her mother, even though Douglas had urged her to call her that.

When Melinda had been fifteen, her grandmother died.

Dolores was the only one who had kept in contact with her over the years. Until she was twelve Douglas had sent some money for Christmas. In most instances, the check from her father was for one hundred dollars. However, this past Christmas, Esmirelda had sent a letter and a check telling Melinda that Douglas was now in Egypt and wouldn't be able to come. Melinda was so disappointed she tore up the check.

"Hurry up, Melinda," Dolly called, "Jimmy is here with the car to take us to the church."

Jimmy Snow had been dating Melinda for all of her senior year. Melinda was glad for the attention but even after heavy petting sessions with Jimmy she wondered whether she loved him. Jimmy was going to Harvard in the fall. His father was the best lawyer in town, everybody said, and his mother a pediatrician. Melinda knew they didn't like him dating her. It had been clear the only time he'd invited her for lunch at his house. They were polite but not at all friendly. She knew they didn't like her.

Melinda and Dolly hopped into the new red Ford convertible Jimmy had gotten as a graduation present. The top was down and it looked out of place in Dolly's neighborhood. Jimmy reached over to kiss her before starting the car. Melinda clung tightly to the cap on her lap during the short trip. She was glad her hair was short, as the wind tossed it to and fro. Jimmy pulled up in front of the church and opened the door for them both. He was carrying his gown in a box and hastened to the rear of the parking lot where the class was assembled for the procession.

Half hoping, Melinda glanced at the people going into the church. Perhaps her father would show up after all, or maybe Richard's foster mother would let him come. She knew he went to a nearby school but hadn't seen him in years so she didn't even know how he'd look. She waved to Dolly as she went also to the back of the church. Melinda was now almost six feet tall and marched at the rear of the line of twenty-three girls. She'd have to sit in the front anyway across from Don Snyder who was giving the farewell address.

When the graduation was over Jimmy had asked Melinda to go with him to a traveling circus. He knew that it had always been her dream to perform with a circus. Before, Melinda had gotten so tall she had pictured herself as a trapeze artist, now she just wanted to be some part of what seemed a glamorous life. Jimmy's parents had planned a graduation party in the evening but Melinda knew she would feel uncomfortable there and shunned.

By two o'clock both of them had changed and were waiting in line for tickets for the afternoon performance. The circus tent and surrounding animal cages were in a field that belonged to the county. In the rear of the tent were some small hills gradually leading to the mountains where few homes had been built. Most of the nearby land was used for farming and the crops were already beginning to shoot up. The year before when the circus was located here one of the animals had gotten loose and trampled over a large field of corn before it was captured.

After a very long wait, one of the clowns arrived and started selling tickets. When Jimmy handed him the money, the clown grumbled that this wasn't his job and this was the third time this week he'd had to substitute selling tickets.

Since there was still time before the performance, Melinda walked over to where the animal cages and tethered animals stood. She patted a camel and was rewarded with an attempt to kick her. Not deterred, she moved over to the two ponies and started picking up some hay and held it out for them to eat. The keeper came by and yelled, "Don't feed the animals! I'll have a hard time sweeping up in the tent if they get a lot to eat now."

Jimmy had drifted off to look at the lone lion and bear.

Melinda spoke up, "Hey mister, I'm sorry about feeding them but you see I've always wanted to be in the circus and I didn't know they shouldn't be fed now."

The keeper, Tom Koplotnick, looked around. The tall girl looked and reminded him of the lad he'd had to help with the animals until an aunt had tracked the boy down and made him go back home two towns ago. There were always some kids around who wanted to join the circus. Perhaps this girl would be strong enough to fill one of the roustabout jobs.

"Can you give me a hand?" he asked, pointing to a large barrel that had to be rolled into the tent for the performance.

Melinda's face lit up and she lifted the heavy barrel over her head and said, "Where do you want it?" This might not be being in the circus but it was close to it.

Tom pointed to the rear of the tent and shook his head. None of the other helpers he'd had could lift anything as heavy, or seemed so willing. "Do you really want to be in the circus?" he asked. "We're shorthanded right now and it is only the middle of the season. We could use someone until we go to Florida for the winter. How old are you? Can't have your family coming after you and dragging you away. You have to be at least eighteen."

Melinda lied, "I'm eighteen, going on nineteen and all through school. I'm going to be kicked out of my foster home any day now."

She would be eighteen in only a few weeks anyway and it was worth it to lie if she could be a part of the circus as she had always dreamed. Little did she realize that being a roustabout meant putting up and taking down the tent almost every twenty-four hours and many other odd jobs any of the circus people had that needed doing. Taking tickets, scrubbing out animal cages to boot.

"Can you start now?" Tom, anxious not to lose the

opportunity urged, "I'll try you out for this performance. What's your name?"

"Melinda, but I'll have to tell my boyfriend first. I would love to have the job. He's over there looking at the lion. I'll be right back." Melinda put down the barrel and ran out to tell Jimmy her good luck. She hoped that right now meant that she wouldn't have to go to the party tonight.

"Guess what? I've got a job!"

Breathlessly, Melinda ran to where Jimmy was standing. He'd been looking around, wondering where she had gone.

"They want me to start right now so I won't be able to sit with you in the stands. Maybe you can return my ticket and get your money back." She didn't add the part about it only being for the afternoon. She knew she could convince Tom to keep her.

"Melinda, you don't just run off with the circus at the drop of the hat. What will I tell Mrs. Erfer? Where will you be so I can see you? You won't even have an address and you have only the clothing you have on. We have all those summer plans."

"I've got it all figured out," Melinda countered. "Just as soon as the circus is over this afternoon you can go and get Mrs. Erfer to pack my scruffy things into that small bag I've been using for track practice and bring it back to me so that I can help at the evening performance."

Jimmy frowned. He knew that Melinda had had this desire for a long time but things were happening too fast. Had she been so worried about not having a home that this was the only way she could escape? He shook his head but agreed to do as Melinda asked. Her glorious smile as she ran back to tell Tom was one that Jimmy had never seen. Although few people knew she was a foster child, she had shared with him some of the stories of the succession of homes where she had been mistreated. He didn't know of her medical problems.

He was surprised when Mrs. Erfer handed him a large bottle of red-and-white capsules, along with the clothing Melinda had requested.

"Tell Melinda I understand, and I hope she'll be happy working in the circus. She certainly has had this in the back of her head for a long time. But, be sure to tell her not to forget to take her medicine regularly. It's very important."

The afternoon had gone by in a pleasant blur for Melinda. Moving equipment in and out of the tent as the acts proceeded made it impossible to see much of what was happening in the single ring, but the excitement was so high and the bustle and timing so fast that Melinda was swept up with the realization that she was really a part of the circus.

To the rhythm of the circus music over and over again to herself she repeated, "I'm really doing it. I'm really doing it. How lucky I am to finally be where I always wanted."

Because she was so eager, all the tasks Tom asked her to do were done swiftly and accurately. Tom began to realize he'd made an offer to the right person.

After the spectators had filed out of the tent, things were set up for the evening performance. Tom motioned to Melinda to follow him.

They walked back to the front of the tent and he talked to the man who had been the ringmaster. Melinda heard the ringmaster protesting. "We can't have a female roustabout, it will cause trouble with the other men."

"We had Lucy early in the spring. This girl is strong and smart; didn't have to tell her twice what to do. Please let me give her a try. If after a week it doesn't work out I'll fire her. We'll still be close enough to Dimsdale that she could hop a bus home."

Tom knew she would be a good worker and to have one who had brains was an added bonus. He'd forgotten that

Lucy had eloped with another roustabout and had left him short two hands.

The ringmaster, George Mays, wiped his forehead with his sleeve. Up close his face appeared wrinkled and his body now assumed a slump. He was tired and weary of constantly coping with being shorthanded. He was too tired to argue. He just nodded and muttered, "We'll give it a week!" He lifted his head and stared at Melinda. "You'd better be good! I'll be watching you! Come on, let's go get some grub."

The two men started for the rear of the tent, Melinda a few steps behind. She could overhear talk about the "gate" and problems with the next stop. She wondered if this meant she'd be kept on for only a week but she was still so excited she skipped the last few steps and entered into the small tent at the rear that served as dressing room and kitchen and dining room. Many of the performers were still in costume since the evening show started at 6:30. Melinda hesitated until Tom beckoned her to follow him through the serving line.

Several heads turned as she brought her filled plate to the long trestle table and sat down next to Tom. One of the clowns winked at her and she felt less self-conscious. Tom hastened to introduce her to the eight others. The girl next to Melinda turned away and continued to talk to the slim young acrobat next to her. In a few days Melinda would get the message that some of the performers ignored roustabouts even though they were essential to the performances. Roustabouts weren't performers!

The two clowns opposite had removed part of their makeup and kept up a bantering conversation with Tom. Melinda felt left out but was so fascinated by what she was observing that she kept smiling. The food was remarkably good. Everyone ate quickly and when finished went back to the counter, rinsed their plate, and placed it on an improvised drain. Tom told Melinda she could wander around for a while but to meet him promptly at six so that they could once again follow the same routine of helping with equipment during the evening show.

Suddenly, Melinda felt alone. Even though everything was fascinating, all the people who milled about had specific jobs and she still didn't know just what her job was or where she would sleep. She saw some of them going into trailers which were parked in the rear of the tents. There were many huge trucks that she assumed were for moving the animals and tents.

A man who she had helped move some of the heavy cages during the afternoon show tapped Melinda on the shoulder.

"Hi, I'm Charlie," he said. "You did a fine job this afternoon. Are you going to be one of Tom's 'boys'? We sure need an extra hand. You sure can heft a load. Where did you learn to move so fast?"

Charlie Long was short, muscular, dark and about forty. He'd been with the circus since he was sixteen. He was married to one of the souvenir sellers and one of his daughters was a horseback rider, the other daughter had married when they were in Florida last winter. Melinda had noticed he knew the routine during the show and when she'd observed he needed help she had automatically lent a hand without being asked.

"I suppose I'm strong because I've been on the track team and learning to throw the shot and do the long jump. I won the interstate competition this year.. I was hoping that someone would give me a scholarship to college but it didn't happen. I hope I can stay with the circus. Looks like they are giving me a one-week trial. I've been wondering though where I will sleep tonight."

"Come on along with me. I'd like you to meet Hilda and Shelly. We live in that bright green trailer with the black trim and red and yellow wheels. 'If you travel with the circus' I

126

always say, 'you should be bright and showy.' We all try to take some time between shows to 'get a load off.' It will be almost midnight when we strike the tent and you'll be busy until then once the evening gets going. Some of the rousts sleep in the trucks. I don't know what Tom has in mind for you."

As they walked the short distance to the trailer, Charlie kept pointing to the various trailers and telling Melinda who lived in them and some of the gossip about the inhabitants. Thus she learned the ringmaster lived with the manager's daughter but that they weren't married. Tom lived by himself. The other names she didn't recognize but was amazed at the comments Charlie was making. It was like listening to Joan in the locker room dishing dirt on all the movie stars. Only this gossip was about circus "stars," performers who Melinda had for years idolized had real families and real problem, too.

The door to the bright green trailer was open and a small fan was blowing the curtain.

"Hilda," Charlie called, "I've brought you Tom's latest addition. The one I told you was so helpful."

Hilda Long came from the rear of the trailer. She had a long brown braid twisted around her head and overdone makeup, concealing her age.

Melinda speculated that the woman must be near fifty. She was wearing a halter top and a long gypsy-like skirt and lots of bangles on her arms. A young girl in jeans poked her head out of a partitioned curtain. "Wow," Shelly whistled. "Boy, are you tall. I'm Shelly. I ride a horse in the show. You goin' to be with the show?"

"Hi," Hilda nodded toward a seat and took one opposite herself. "How old are you, kid? Don't look as though you're old enough to shack up with the circus."

Hilda had never been one to mince words and Charlie glared darkly at her to shut her up. Melinda was taken aback.

127

After Charlie's friendly greeting she had expected his wife would be more affable. She looked around the trailer, which was larger than she had imagined from the outside.

Obviously it wasn't new, the upholstery was worn, but everything was neat and clean. Not showy, as the outside would have indicated, but rather on the dull side in browns and tans. She could see the small kitchen had been scrubbed until it shone

Shelly came out of her "room" and sat in the driver's seat and started a conversation without giving Melinda time to reply to Hilda's questioning. "I'm glad Tom has hired a girl for a change. Girls can do just as much as men but we have a tough time proving it, don't we?"

"I've never thought about it much." Melinda liked this girl who was short like Charlie with blonde curly hair. She had observed that the tricks that Shelly did on her horse were much harder than the other men who rode horses in the show.

"Where are you going to sleep tonight?" Shelly asked. "It wouldn't be fair for Tom to put you in one of the trucks with the other guys. Mom, maybe she could sleep here. There's an extra bunk now that sis isn't here. I'd like the company." Shelly winked at Melinda. She missed her sister and this tall girl looked so abashed at her mother's brusqueness that she wanted to make it up to her.

Hilda didn't reply but glanced over to Charlie as if to ask him his opinion. Finally she said, "I guess your father will have to make that decision after he talks with Tom." She wasn't too pleased at Shelly's suggestion, however. Hilda didn't think it wise to have the girl sleep with the other roustabouts. She wished Shelly had asked her privately and not put her into such a spot.

"Why don't you relax here until set-up, time?" Charlie suggested to Melinda. "I'll stop by Tom's trailer and get his okay in a little while. Would you like a Coke?" He stepped over to a small fridge and got out a beer for himself.

"No, thanks." Melinda felt uncomfortable and as though she was intruding, but soon Shelly was busy showing her how the bunk at the front of the trailer slid down to make another bed in case they had five sleeping in the trailer. The family started jabbering about the next small town they would travel to during the early morning. They remembered it specially because there had been a large generous crowd the previous year. It was easy to surmise that this was important to Hilda since her sales of souvenirs would go up if there were a lot of people.

"Do you always follow the same route each year?" Melinda inquired. "Do you know where you'll be next week this time?" If she had to be let go at the end of the week perhaps she could arrange for Jimmy to pick her up.

"Want to look at the schedule?" Charlie asked, rummaging around in the dash board of the trailer. He handed Melinda a rumpled sheet of paper with the dates and towns listed for the whole season.

According to the list, the circus had started at the end of April in Tennessee, gone through Virginia, Delaware, Pennsylvania and after New York would go on to New Jersey, and North and South Carolina. The last date on the list was in October, then in large letters, FLORIDA was printed. Except for a few nearby towns Melinda didn't recognize the names of the places they would be stopping. In most of the towns they would be having two shows then move on to the next town. There didn't seem to be any days when there wouldn't be a performance. She did notice that in a week they would be near Albany.

"It looks like they keep you busy going from town to town," she remarked. She handed the list back to Charlie.

"We have to hit the small towns that the large circuses can't stop at. We're just a small outfit. There are fewer and fewer small circuses left. One that tours the Midwest, and one that tours the Southwest are the only ones I know of. Soon there won't be any of us left. I feel sorry for the smalltown kids that will never get taken to the large cities to see a circus. It is getting too expensive to put on the small town shows. It's harder and harder to find talent to work for what we can pay and harder and harder to get kids like you who will work for next to nothing just to be part of the show."

Melinda hadn't thought about what she might be paid. She'd been so excited that she would be having a chance to be a part of the circus she hadn't until now given it any consideration. She knew that she could have a job in one of the stores during the summer if she'd stayed in Dimsdale. A friend of Dolly's who managed the supermarket told her that he'd pay her $4.00 an hour. She didn't think this was the right time to ask just how much she would be getting. In fact, she didn't really care.

The sound of an alarm bell interrupted the conversation.

"Fifteen minutes to set-up time."

Shelly dashed for her room to change into her costume. Hilda hastily gathered the bottles and straightened the trailer. Charlie excused himself.

"If I want to catch Tom I'd better get a move-on! I'm going to ask him to put Melinda on my 'team' so that you'll just have to follow my directions and not wait for him tonight. I'll get it straight about your sleeping arrangements, too. I think Shelly would be happy to have you as a bunk mate."

Melinda smiled as she looked around the empty living room in the front of the trailer. Already she felt at home. Shelly came out dressed for her performance in a short pale blue full skirt over a darker blue leotard suit. There was gold braid in an elaborate design over both the skirt and leotard. She had twisted her hair on top of her head and she had a blue butterfly perched jauntily on one side. During the show in the afternoon Melinda had had only a glance as Shelly had spun by on her horse doing cartwheels and headstands. Now Melinda admired the attention that had gone into designing the costume.

"You look terrific. I would like to be able to be one of the performers someday, but for now I'm glad that Tom has asked me to help with the moving. Do they sometimes have one of the roustabouts act in the show?"

"If you sell tickets they might let you put on some clown makeup." Shelly frowned. *If this girl believed she'd gotten her foot in the door to do performing she'd be sadly disappointed,* she thought.

"I don't have to go on for another half hour, but we all march in the opening parade. Come on, we'll have to be lining up soon and you'll be needed. As each act is finished in the evening performance their equipment and animals are loaded in the big trucks so you'll be very busy."

Both girls left the trailer and proceeded to the rear of the circus tent. Cars were busy parking and a long line was waiting for tickets. Tom rushed past, calling over his shoulder that it was his turn to sell tickets and that Melinda should do what Charlie told her to do until he came back.

Once the parade that started the show was over, the pace quickened. Suddenly there were four men that hadn't been helping Charlie during the afternoon hustling props and animals into the trucks. Melinda didn't have time to ask where they'd been in the afternoon. Later she would find that they doubled as truck drivers and worked setting up the tents in the morning and then slept most of the day. Three of them were almost as young as she was but one was as old as Charlie. He was tall, bald and obviously the boss. As he barked orders the others hefted, pulled, pushed and shoved things up the ramps of the trucks, which were

131

now backed up close to the rear tent opening.

By ten, almost all the cars of the spectators had gone and already the elephants were inside the tent helping pull down the large poles. Charlie was directing those holding the lines and handed one end to Melinda.

"Hold on tight, don't let it get slack. Brace your legs and don't let go until I tell you."

Melinda clung to the heavy rope. She wished she had gloves like she saw most of the men had. The rope was rough and hard to keep taut, particularly when the top began to collapse. She had time to look around at what was happening. Men were at the ends of all the ropes suspended from the sides of the tent. Gradually as the poles went down, Tom and Charlie directed the folding of the sections and after they were all down on the ground the men who had been holding the ropes helped lift the sections into one of the trucks.

It was now past twelve and as the last of the trucks shut its rear doors Tom came by.

"Melinda, Charlie asked if you could ride with him. It's okay with me. Remember, for the time being he'll be your boss but I'll be keeping an eye on you too. See you in Birdsboro tomorrow. By the way, someone left a bag for you when I was taking tickets. I gave it to Charlie."

Charlie's trailer was only one of three trailers left in the open field. Melinda began to feel the toll of the long day catching up with her as she walked slowly across the rutted ground. Her hands were sore and she wondered if she'd gotten blisters, but in the dark she couldn't see. Lights were shining from the trailers and the headlights of the departing trucks gave a glow. It was hard to imagine that only a few hours before the field had been well lit and crowded with noisy people.

"Hurry up," Shelly said as Melinda opened the door of the trailer. "It's my turn to drive. You can sleep in my bunk tonight. I've put your bag in there," she said, pointing to the curtain where she'd changed that afternoon

"Mom and Pop are probably already turned in. We take turns driving so every third night they have time to sleep together. Do you drive? It would be a help. I'll probably get only about four hours' sleep before I have to go on tomorrow. If you need to use the bathroom don't flush. And don't shower until tomorrow when we are hooked up to a water line. Our tank is almost empty."

The engine started up before Melinda had time to sit down on the bunk. She was unprepared for the lights to go out and had to grope around to find her bag. She wanted a bath and a change of clothing but had to settle for a fresh shirt. As she felt around in the bag the medicine that Dolly had packed fell into her hand. How was she going to manage? She'd have to skip her nighttime dose and take doubles in the morning. She had hoped she would have seen Jimmy when he came with the bag to say good-bye. She would just have to find time to call him in the morning. She had no idea how to turn on a faucet or where to find a glass in the dark. A small night light glowed in the hall but there wasn't enough light to see in these unfamiliar surroundings. She didn't want to bother Shelly or draw her attention to the fact she needed medicine. She did know that she couldn't miss many pills without having a seizure.

It didn't take long to go to sleep. The movement of the trailer and the steady hum of the engine somehow reminded her of when her grandmother had rocked and sang her to sleep. At six, when the sun started to shine through the window over her bunk, Melinda awakened as the trailer bumped over rough terrain and came to a squeaking halt. Looking out of the window she could see the large trucks already starting to unload. Now she was conscious of the aches in her back, arms and legs as she stretched. Staring at her grimy hands she

133

saw that indeed she had developed a blister on her palm where she'd been holding the rope.

Shelly poked her head around the curtain. "Ready to give me a turn?" she asked. "I stopped and filled up our water tank so you can have a shower if you want."

"Thanks, I certainly can use one. What do I do with my dirty clothing? And what do I do about breakfast?"

"Just pile your dirty stuff in this laundry bag with mine. Jessie, the cotton candy lady, takes our wash to a laundromat every couple of days. She does the wash for a lot of us trailer people. We pay her a couple of bucks a month. The cook tent won't be set up for another hour or so. We keep some cereal and bread in the kitchen. If you're not fussy you can have breakfast here. Sometimes it is easier. There's instant coffee. The stove is gas. Just be quiet about it so that all of us can get another forty winks."

Melinda would have liked to have had another forty winks as well but didn't feel it fair, after Shelly had driven all night, to ask where she'd sleep when Shelly wasn't driving. She took her bag and went into the small bath and took a shower. She felt refreshed but still ached. Filling a glass she took three capsules with some juice she found in the tiny refrigerator. She ate two slices of bread with some jam that she found on a shelf and went outside to watch the bustle as the drivers again set up the tents with the help of the elephants and other roustabouts. They were being directed by the eldest driver.

Tom's trailer had still not arrived. Several of the other trailers were already parked. This time they were setting up in a large field beside a church. Streets with medium-sized houses surrounded the church in all directions. It was as though the church was the hub of the community. In a distance were large buildings and factories. It was obviously larger than Dimsdale.

Melinda could see some families with children had come to watch. They had parked on the church parking lot and were keeping back some distance from the trucks. By eight there would be a parade through town to publicize the performances. Right now there were still trailers pulling into the lot and a few people who had arrived earlier wandering about. Melinda recognized one of the clowns that had been opposite from her at dinner go into the smaller tent which was already up. She followed, since she knew this was where they put on make-up. Perhaps she could see him do his.

Inside the tent she was surprised to see the clown putting out fruit and starting the coffee machine.

He turned when he saw her and said, "Hi, it's too early for breakfast unless you will settle for a banana and milk. It is my job to help with the breakfast set up. Want to help? Can you fry bacon?"

Melinda had always been happy to help in the kitchen so she pitched in and soon was frying pounds and pounds of bacon and sausage and helping set out the buns, which had just come from the local bakery. She snatched a sweet roll and ate as she worked. Unknowingly she had gotten herself one of the additional jobs at which almost all of the circus people doubled.

When Tom arrived forty minutes later he stood and watched Melinda as she scurried, helping set up the trestle tables. He smiled to himself and mentally patted himself on the back for having hired such a willing worker. He knew that she had volunteered to help since Charlie wasn't anywhere to be seen.

"I'm glad to see you're making yourself useful," Tom said. "Is it possible to get some coffee and a bun to go? I have to supervise some of the line-up for the parade and make sure all those animals are unloaded. I want to eat on the run."

"Sure," Binky the clown replied. "Due to Melinda's extra

help this morning we're ready early. Can I have her every morning? You don't have to tell her twice what to do. Came right in and pitched in and hasn't stopped for a minute."

"You'll have to part with her now. Melinda, go make sure Charlie is up. We all have to get busy. Sure, Binky, she can help until I need her every morning," Tom tossed over his shoulder as he beckoned for Melinda to follow him.

Days began to assume a similar pattern. Melinda never realized at what point the excitement turned into deadly routine, but by September it no longer seemed so much fun to get up early to help with breakfast and spend all day lugging heavy objects from here to there and back again. She still felt like a fifth wheel in Charlie's trailer. Even though Shelly made her feel at home, Hilda never made her feel welcome. Every week she tried to call Jimmy but he was seldom home. His mother would say she'd give him the message. Once and a while she'd call Mrs. Erfer.

Dolly Erfer had driven to Connecticut and surprised her one afternoon. She had a new bottle of Dilantin and was amazed at how brown and muscular Melinda had become. It was good to see someone from home. Melinda didn't have much time after the afternoon performance but they did have a nice chat. Dolly had brought her two presents. One was from Jimmy. Melinda's birthday back in July had gone uncelebrated. Back in the trailer Melinda opened Jimmy's present. She started to cry when she saw the pale pink satin blouse. It was one she had admired in a store window the last time they'd gone out. Certainly not the kind of clothing she now had to wear.

By the end of October most of the trucks were headed south for Florida. Some of the roustabouts had already headed home. Because Melinda slept in Charlie's trailer she had never had to ride in the trucks, but now Tom told her she would have to ride in a truck with the animals since they would need feeding during the trip. Melinda knew Ralph the driver, who was, she guessed, only a year or two older than herself. He was tall, dark and considered himself handsome but tended to get surly if anyone crossed him. He'd tried to make passes at most of the girl performers with little success. Melinda wasn't too happy about the arrangement.

Now that there wasn't another show to set up, all of the trucks took off separately. Ralph smiled as she slid into the seat next to him. Normally there would have been three in the front but the other two boys had left back in South Carolina. Melinda tried to keep up a conversation with Ralph who talked at length about a girl he knew down in Florida that he had shacked up with the previous winter. Traffic on Route One was light and Melinda was surprised when by ten o'clock Ralph pulled into a rest stop and suggested that they both sleep. Since Melinda couldn't drive, she realized that their truck would probably be the last one to arrive at winter headquarters.

"Can't we stop at a motel?" Melinda didn't want to sleep in the back of the cab with Ralph. "I'll pay for it."

"Naw, it's about fifty miles to the nearest town. I haven't seen a motel for a long time." Ralph put his hand on Melinda's knee. "What's the matter kid? Afraid old Ralph Boy is too good for you? I'm gentle as a lamb." He leaned over and quickly kissed Melinda on the lips.

"I've been looking at you all summer. The way your perky breasts move when you lift something heavy has been driving me nuts." To accompany his suggestive remark, he moved both hands over Melinda's breasts and again kissed her.

"Cut it out, Ralph!" Melinda pushed Ralph's hands away and slid to the far corner of the seat. She searched the parking lot, looking for other vehicles. Except for what looked like an empty bus 100 yards away, the lot was deserted. Suddenly she realized that there wasn't any support nearby and that she had to defend herself. "I can sleep in the cab. You take the bunk. I don't kiss on my first date," she said sarcastically but in a joking tone.

In the dark it was hard to tell what kind of expression Ralph had. Melinda had seen his scowls when someone bumped into him accidentally. She had seen him on occasion deliberately trip the culprit or take a swing that decked the miscreant. He was taller, heavier and stronger than she was. All she could hope for was that she could convince him she wasn't interested in his advances.

"Hop over into the bunk," Ralph growled. "Think you're too good for me, do you? I'll show you this is no 'date' sister. You're not the first dame I've laid in the back of this cab, and don't think you can scream or get away. Just wait till you see the size of my prick, long and heavy, the kind most girls swoon over."

By now Melinda realized Ralph was in earnest. His huge hands were tugging at her legs, trying to toss her over into the back of the cab. Melinda pushed and scratched as he managed to half lift, half drag her squirming body over the back of the high seat. Before she had time to roll he had hopped over on top of her and began sliding her shirt up and over her head.

"Don't, don't! I don't want you to touch me! Please Ralph, Tom won't like this at all."

Ralph started to laugh. "I told Tom you had the hots for me, that's why he gave you the job to ride with me. He'll never believe you." Ralph was busy holding her down with one arm and sliding her jeans down over her hips with his other.

The rape took only a few minutes. Melinda screamed and couldn't stop screaming even when Ralph withdrew and hopped back over the seat. She could feel blood trickling down her leg from her vagina. Ralph leaned over and hit her, hard, on the side of the head to shut her up.

She stopped screaming and felt her body go rigid. Fleetingly, she knew she was going to have a seizure but blackness soon blanked out any conscious thought.

Ralph, relieved that she had stopped screaming, didn't look over again but took out a pack of cigarettes and searched around in the cab for his pint of bourbon. After a few snorts he began to sing. "Way down south, in the land of cotton. Good times there are not forgotten." He laughed. "How about another round? Think you could keep quiet this time?"

When he leaned over the seat he could feel that Melinda was bunched up in a fetal position. She didn't stir when he grabbed her breast hard, neither did she protest. Feeling he was accepted he again tried to climb on top of her but her rigid body remained curled. "Oh, like it from the back this time?" he exclaimed, inserting his cock into the limp body. "You liked it after all, didn't you."

Ralph was removing his penis when Melinda began to stir. He curled up next to her back and suddenly became aware that the bunk was soaking wet. He had no way of knowing that at the beginning of the seizure Melinda's bladder had emptied. "You slut, wetting my bed." He cuffed Melinda on the side of the head so hard that she again sank into unconsciousness.

It was beginning to turn light when she finally came to. She stared at her bruised arm and knew by the feel of her tongue she had had a seizure. Gradually as she awakened more fully the memory of the rape came back in bits and pieces. She had a hard time figuring out where she was. She did remember Ralph! Where was he? On the shelf above the bunk was her carry-all bag. She lifted it down and searched for some clothing. Trying to avoid the large wet spot she slid out of her jeans and panties. She knew this

139

happened when she had a seizure. She hadn't had one in several years and guessed she'd become careless about taking her medicine.

Glancing around the parking lot, she saw several cars nearby. Although it was early, Melinda hoped she could hop a ride with one of them. She didn't want to spend the next 300 miles with Ralph. She'd try to get to Florida on a bus if necessary. Reaching into the side of her bag for her cache of money Melinda came up empty handed. The sound of the lion in the rear of the truck reminded her that she had promised to feed him and the horses they were transporting. Quickly she got out and went to the rear of the truck. Ralph had already opened it up and stood above her inside the truck, calmly feeding hay to one of the horses.

From the ground Ralph appeared even larger and taller than Melinda remembered. The sudden realization of intense hatred and violation plus the stench of the unclean animals stalls triggered intense nausea. Doubling over beside the truck Melinda retched again and again. Leaning over had started the dizziness she associated with a seizure. Unable to control her body she slumped to the asphalt.

Ralph glanced at her inert body, shrugged, and kept feeding the horses. He opened the small ice chest and got out the daily ration of meat for the lion and pushed it through the bars of his cage. Part of Melinda's job was to clean the stalls and cages. That wasn't what Ralph had bargained on doing.

"Come on, quit stalling and get up here and do the damn cleaning," Ralph yelled but there was no response. He hopped down from the tail gate and noticed that Melinda was lying with her hair and face in the vomit from her stomach. Once again there was a small puddle beneath her buttocks. Ralph swung his leg and kicked her legs, trying to waken her. He noticed her tongue was bleeding and protruding from her month. By now she had stopped the violent shaking but appeared pale and sleepy.

"Hell girl, what a mess!" By now a few children had come round the side of the truck and were peeking inside at the horses. The lion cage was situated beyond the stalls but the roar was unmistakable.

"What's the matter with the girl?" one of the boys asked.

"I guess she had something that didn't agree with her. She'll be okay in a little while. Just go away and don't bother us."

"You're a circus truck, aren't you? Where are you going?" a small girl in a yellow jump suit asked.

"We're all done for the summer and going to Florida for the winter." Ralph didn't want any more questions. He wanted the children to disappear, but to his dismay an older man rounded the front of the truck, coming toward Ralph from the opposite side. He stopped when he saw Melinda.

"Linda, you and Paul go get in the car. We're ready to go now. What's the matter with the girl? I'm an orderly in a hospital in Greensboro. She looks mighty sick to me. Do you want me to get my wife? She's a nurse, maybe she can help."

"Naw, she'll be fine. Must have been the smell of the animals after they've been shut up all night. I'll take care of her." Ralph reluctantly picked Melinda up.

He tried to prop her up on the front seat of the cab. Her body was limp, and smelling her hair had turned his stomach when he carried her. Looking at her slumped body, Ralph only felt annoyance. Gone was all the lust from the previous night. Too callous for remorse or pity he was only disgusted that she now presented a problem he didn't want. For ten minutes he stood beside the truck hoping she would rouse then he returned to the rear of the truck, shut the tail gate and doors. He'd have to start driving if he was to make it to Sarasota by dark today. He slid into the cab, pushing Melinda's body roughly along the seat.

By the time he reached a truck stop where he could stop for breakfast Melinda was starting to waken. She lay still though so that Ralph wouldn't know it. The odor of the vomit had permeated the whole cab even though the windows were open, and as she opened her eyes a slit she could see that her hair was full of debris. As the truck parked next to another semi, Ralph got out. For a few minutes he was gone but soon was back with a large bucket of water. He swung her head out the side of the cab and threw the water over her head. He had hoped this would waken her and wash some of the offending stuff from her hair and face.

Still not wanting Ralph to know she was awake, Melinda stayed quiet with her eyes closed. The shock of the cold water made her intensely aware of the aches in her arms, tongue, legs and stomach. Once more the revulsion of the rape swept through her and the determination to escape started to form in her still-foggy consciousness.

Ralph cuffed her head with his closed fist. "Wake up, damn you. I'm going to breakfast. You'd better be awake when I get back. Not only did you smell up this whole cab but those animals in the back have to be cleaned, too."

As soon as Melinda was sure Ralph was inside the diner she sat up and looked around. How could she get away? There were four other trucks parked nearby. Reaching to get her bag she opened the door and slid down to the ground. Her legs felt like rubber but she managed to scoot around the truck next to theirs and was delighted to see that the next truck had a New York license. Not only that, the tail gate was open and crates piled halfway back. It looked like an ideal hiding place. If she was lucky it would be headed to New York and she could be home in a day or two.

142

Finding it easy to jiggle one of the crates, Melinda made just enough room for herself between two tall crates marked A.B.C. Trucking and sat down to try to repair the damage to her hair. The water had soaked it and using the comb diligently she managed to get it looking fairly neat.

10

Tinker

St. Louis at the end of October was having a miserable spell of rainy weather. Evening came earlier and earlier now, and the sky hadn't been seen in ten days. It seemed semi-dark all the time. Water poured down relentlessly. Sometimes in a torrent, other times in a drizzle, but never seeming to stop completely. Thus the figures dashing across the streets going to the warehouse district huddled against the damp and cold. For along with the rain it had turned cold, leaving the streets coated with ice early in the mornings.

Tinker was looking forward to a hot shower and a regular bed at the end of this run. He and Swat had been on the road steadily for the past week. First from Albuquerque to Dallas and then on to Atlanta picking up any load they could find. Sometimes with a full load, most, like this one, half full. Being an independent trucker was getting to be harder and harder. The profit on this trip would just about pay the overdue insurance.

But this was St. Louis. Mary Beth Parker had made him comfortable more than once in her large round bed with the red velvet curtains. Tinker was already feeling anxious to get this load out of the semi and himself out of the cold. He'd find a load going south in a few days.

Swat came round the front of the truck. Tinker had been negotiating with the dispatcher inside the office. "You'd better come out and see what I found between the crates when I started to unload."

"I'm trying to arrange a load on Wednesday," Tinker glared at Swat. "I'll be out when I'm damn good and ready."

Carefully, Swat removed the cases in front of the unconscious body. He bent over and felt the wrist of the prone figure. With a deep sigh he realized that he'd been afraid, because of the stench, that someone had stashed a dead body in their truck. At least the person was breathing, although shallowly.

"What's all the rush about? What was in the truck?" Tinker called from the rear of the truck.

"Come on in here! Someone tried to hitch a ride and was hiding between the crates. He's knocked out and seems like he is sick. I think we'd better call for an ambulance."

"Can't do that. We'd be in a heap of trouble with the insurance company. They're just itching to cancel my policy as it is. We'll dump him at the emergency room of that hospital near Mary's."

Swat frowned but didn't answer. He got back in the cab and waited sullenly until Tinker completed the unloading of the rig. Together they moved the limp body into the cab and discovered that it wasn't a "him" in the process. Tinker had a vague sense that he had seen the girl's face before. It had been a long time and many escapades since he had left when he'd set fire to the Erfers' house. Melinda still had the same facial features but of course had matured so the identification and link to his past was fleeting. The drive to the hospital was short, fortunately, because the smell coming from the hunched-over girl made them drive with their windows open. The rain had again started pelting down hard and came in on Swat's side.

Instead of pulling into the emergency drive Tinker pulled up to the curb fifty feet from the entrance. "Pull her out and put her over by that tree," he directed Swat.

"I thought we were going to take her inside," Swat protested.

"I told you I don't want any trouble with the insurance company. If we take her in they will want our names and try to nail us for some money. They might even blame us for the way she is. Somebody will find her and take her inside. Hurry up. I don't want anyone to see us dumping her."

"You'll have to give me a hand," Swat had grabbed Melinda under the arms and was tugging to get her out the door.

"Just bounce her out and drag her. I'm not getting out in this rain."

Accustomed to Tinker's temper, Swat gave a big pull and Melinda's feet made a quick descent from the high seat. Her weight made Swat lose his balance and he fell into the gutter. Tinker started to curse and reluctantly came around and helped prop Melinda up against the nearby tree.

"Get your frickin' body up in that cab, quick," he commanded.

"You've got the feelin' of a snake," Swat replied. He'd been thinking of ditching Tinker for a long time and hoped that in the two-day layover he'd be able to find another trucker who'd be better to work for. No Mary Beth Parker for him. He generally stayed at the "Y" or a motor court.

"Drive me to that motor court near the warehouses. I'll meet you there on Wednesday." Swat added to himself, *If I don't find somebody else to take me on before then.*

Almost three hours went by until, at the change of shifts, one of the nurses found Melinda and went back to have someone bring a gurney to carry her inside.

Two days later Melinda awakened to a familiar nightmare. An intravenous tube in her arm and the click of the inflated stockings around her legs. It was hours before she fully remembered the rape and what had happened when she hid in the truck and the fact she had been very hungry.

Now, how had she gotten here? What was the matter? So many questions. Where was she? Would Tom be concerned when she didn't show up in Florida? Or perhaps would anyone know she was here? What was wrong with her? Why the I.V.?

When a resident came to check on her all of this spilled out in a long torrent. George Bliss was in his last year of residency in neurology and pleased this unnamed patient had regained consciousness. He too had a lot of questions about this young girl, who had come out of the cold rain, dehydrated, with a below-normal temperature, a rape victim with tears to her rectum and a seizure disorder. In addition, she had bruises and scratches over most of her body and no identification at all. He'd wondered why someone had been so brutal as to leave her within feet of the emergency room and not bring her inside. There were many questions that even her medical condition left to be answered. Why hadn't she fought the rape? Or had she had the seizure first and someone had taken advantage of her in that state? No matter what, "she" was one of the strangest cases George had seen in all his medical education. He was delighted that she was regaining consciousness and could answer some of the mysterious reasons for her miserable condition.

"You're in Memorial Hospital in St. Louis," he began to explain. "I'm Dr. Bliss. I've been taking care of you because you have a seizure problem. You were found outside of the hospital several days ago and you probably hadn't had anything to drink for a long time. That is why the I.V. is in your arm and since you haven't been conscious there is a catheter to catch your urine. What is your name and where do you live? The police have no record of a missing person so we couldn't let your relatives know where you are."

"My name is Melinda Erfer," she answered automatically. She had adopted Dolly's name for the past five years and had almost forgotten that wasn't her "real" name.

"I had been working with a circus and don't have any address. No one would be looking for me except my boss at the circus maybe." She hesitated because she was sure that Ralph would have told Tom some crazy story to explain why she wasn't with him when he arrived.

Her story had hit the papers and T.V. the evening she was discovered. Once a reporter had seen the police report it had been the featured article on the front page. Swat and Tinker had seen it on the television evening news. Tinker's panic sent him off without waiting for a load. He hoped he'd pick up something in Columbia or Kansas City. He'd not even let Swat know he was going, so on Wednesday when Swat turned up at the terminal, he was shocked to find that Tinker hadn't been there to pick up the load he'd been promised.

The dispatcher was angry. Told Swat to get lost. Now Swat had no job and little chance of getting one right away. On top of that Tinker hadn't paid him in two weeks and Swat was broke. They'd been together for fourteen months and it wasn't unusual for Tinker to hold out money until he got a good-paying haul. Swat was mad. He walked back to the motel and wondered what he was going to do. He turned on the T.V. and watched some game shows until the noon news announced a reward for information from anyone who might know who was responsible for dumping the still-unnamed girl in front of the hospital.

In a flash, Swat knew how he could get back at Tinker, get himself a bankroll and get rid of the guilty sensation that had haunted him. He picked up the phone and called the number that he'd seen flashed on the screen. He told the person who answered that he'd been walking past the hospital on Monday morning and seen a trucker drag a body and stick it by a tree. He then gave the license number of Tinker's truck. They asked him why he hadn't reported it sooner. Swat hadn't anticipated this question. "Just wanted to stay out of somebody else's business. When I saw it on television how bad that girl is I wanted to tell you what I seen. When do I get the money?"

Swat was uncomfortable when he was told that if they picked up the truck and he could identify the man, he'd get his money. However, they assured him that at no time would he be identified as the person who had given the information. So it was wait and hope.

Two days later the police called Swat. They had picked up Tinker in Kansas City. He was being charged with rape, assault, abandonment and six other offenses. Swat was asked to come and identify him in a line-up.

Of course Swat had no difficulty in picking Tinker from the line of five men. Even though the police woman assured Swat there was no way he'd be seen, the palms of his hands were wet and by the time he'd left the building Swat had one of his throbbing headaches. They still hadn't given him any of the promised reward, saying that it was necessary for Melinda to also identify Tinker.

Swat knew that this was impossible. He also knew he'd gotten his neck out too far. Tinker had possibly figured that Swat was the one who had fingered him. There were too many questions that the police were beginning to ask that he had to invent lies to answer. He decided that, money or no money, he'd better get out of St. Louis before Tinker pointed a finger in his direction. He'd used his last dollar to get to the police station. It was downtown and quite a way from his motel. Swat walked for a while in the direction of the motel then spotted the bus terminal.

He'd try to convince Traveler's Aid to buy him a ticket to Chicago. His sister lived there and would put him up until he could get a job if he was lucky.

Things weren't that easy for Tinker. At the preliminary

hearing the judge had asked for $50,000 bail so Tinker went back to a cell knowing there wasn't anyone who'd put up the money for a bail bond. No one had believed his story of finding Melinda unconscious in the rear of the truck trailer. It was with some hope when the judge appointed an attorney to represent him. However, when she appeared it was obvious that the sad plight of Melinda, as told by the papers and media, had prejudiced her. She listened to his story and took down notes but Tinker knew she was skeptical about many points for she had him repeat them over and over. Tinker knew she'd not look hard to find Swat.

The date for the trial was set for February. Tinker wasn't able to convince any of the other inmates at the county jail that he wasn't a rapist either. On several occasions he'd been unable to defend himself physically. This was different from the detention center he'd spent eighteen months in for robbery when he was sixteen. Under his breath he'd frequently murmur, "If I could get my hands on Swat, I'd kill him."

When the case finally came up it didn't take long for the district attorney to convince the jury, judge and spectators, consisting mostly of news persons, that Tinker had done all the nasty deeds that he'd been accused of. He was surprised when his attorney put Dr. Bliss on the stand. She hadn't told Tinker that Dr. Bliss had called her in December. Melinda, after a long period of therapy, had been able to recall that she had climbed into the truck on her own.

Even with Dr. Bliss' testimony that Tinker wasn't the rapist, the rest of the charges were enough to have the jury declare him guilty.

Several days later the judge sentenced him to twelve years with no possibility of parole.

11

Dr. George Bliss

At twenty-eight, George Bliss had been looking forward to his move to San Francisco at the end of his residency in May. His brother, Matt, had by now a large practice in neurology there. Matt was six years older than George. They had both gone to the University of Pennsylvania for their medical degrees. Matt had done his residency at Abington Hospital but had been lucky that Stanford Lane had wanted to add him to their staff.

Matt and Sandy, his wife, had a large house in Walnut Creek and were the very proud parents of twin boys. They had promised George that he could stay with them until he was ready to go on his own. George knew this was going to work out fine until . . .

Melinda. What was it about this patient that he could not let go? Ever since she had come into the hospital his attention had been consumed with an intense desire to heal her. Not only in body but to cushion the damage to her psyche. He found himself talking at length with her nurses and her social worker. At first he'd attributed his interest to pity. After all, Melinda was only a child and to arrive with no clothing, no relatives, a victim of a brutal rape, and as they were gradually beginning to learn horrible neglect of her epilepsy, made more than enough reasons to spark his medical and human interest.

But, there was more. As Melinda regained her strength

and memory, George became fascinated with her intelligence and insight. Because she had no clothing and by the fifth day wanted to get out of bed, he'd supplied her with a set of his own greens. He was there when she stood at the side of the bed and helped her into the long pants and top. When she straightened up, her eyes met his. They were almost the same height.

Melinda was becoming aware of Dr. Bliss as a person as well. Looking into his gray eyes and up at his auburn hair she responded to his broad grin with a wan smile. She felt his gentle arms encouraging her to stand alone but with the assurance that he'd not let go until she had her balance. After a few tentative steps he let go but kept holding her hand until she sat in a nearby chair.

The result of the past week's events left Melinda reluctant to trust people. She felt she had to protect her body from any invasion. Somewhat like the child who had shivered in the coal cellar when she was little, she tried to find some inner warmth to comfort her. Dr. Bliss was different from the others. He seemed to want to shelter her.

When Melinda had first regained consciousness it had taken a long time to sort out exactly what had happened and when. At first the memory of her childhood hospitalization had mingled with the scents and noises until the dimly recessed fright overlapped into the present. It was in this half-wakening state that she became aware of the tall slim doctor who kept coming to tickle her toes frequently. Hours later, when she was fully awake, he was by her bed more than any other person.

The second day that she was conscious a burly, red-faced man, in a dark gray suit came bustling into the room, pad and pencil in hand.

"Hi, little lady, I'm Flip Johnson from the U.P. service. I want to hear all your story. You made quite a splash in the

152

local press. A real tear-jerker. Tell me, who raped you?"

Melinda started to scream. Long piercing screams. Her head jerked back and once again her body went into the twisting motion that always accompanied a seizure. Nurses rushed into the room and began inserting the depressor into her mouth so she wouldn't bite her tongue.

Flip stood back while all this was going on. This was part of the story he'd not heard. He wanted to know more. At this point, George Bliss rushed into the room. Scanning the scene quickly he immediately spotted Flip and surmised the reason for the current panic situation.

"What's the matter with her? All I did was ask her who raped her and she started screaming," Flip inquired.

"Get out of this room! Who let you in? What business do you have disrupting my patient? This is a very sick girl. She doesn't need to deal with any questions like that right now. It's my business to get her well. Hasn't she had enough happen to her?"

Flip scurried out into the hall but turned to face George. "I'm from the U.P. Thought this might make national news and came to check it out. Are you her doctor? What's your name? What do you know about what happened? Has she told you who left her off?"

"You're not getting any information from me, and if I see you around her again I'll call our security people and have you thrown out!" George turned as soon as he saw Flip get on the elevator, to see how bad the present seizure had become.

"Ladies," he said, addressing the several nurses in attendance, "you'll have to be more careful about who gets onto the floor. We may have more curious people from the press coming around and at the present time she's too fragile. I'll try to cope with anyone who's asking questions. Just page me."

Shirley, one of the nurses, winked at both the other women. All of them had noticed Dr. Bliss' extreme interest in this patient. They'd been observing him going in and out of the room. Even on his day off he'd stopped in and stayed by the bed, sitting in the chair, for over an hour. The night nurse had mentioned that he'd even been by in the early morning for the past few days.

Defensively, Shirley answered, "He must have climbed up the stairs. The guard wouldn't let anyone up the elevator without a pass."

"I'll stay here and watch her until she comes out of it. I hear a buzzer going off. Pay attention to 409. He's getting a CT scan at eleven. Seems very agitated about it. I just came from there when I heard the screaming. One of you go in and talk to him about hockey or some sport to take his mind off going down."

Melinda was accustomed to seeing George sitting by her bed when she wakened. It became a great comfort to see him smile. As the days passed and her seizures got under control he would stop by and sit and talk. Sometimes about other patients, sometimes about the upcoming local elections, at other times about tennis, his one sporting interest.

When Melinda had so many questions about his medical terminology he brought her a medical dictionary. This only opened up more questions and he began to bring her more and more articles about epilepsy, her particular curiosity. Before long she began telling him about what had happened to her at an early age and she now could understand what had been happening to her. Some of the descriptions of her treatment by her stepmother were so graphic he wanted to tell Melinda to stop. The stories of what had gone on in the foster homes and the neglect of her medical needs made him more and more angry.

What amazed George was that despite this Melinda displayed more than an average intelligence. She read at a rapid rate and came up with insightful questions about what she read. She seemed able to comprehend the relationships of the complicated neurological systems at times better than the interns on the floor he was supervising.

By the end of the second week, one of the social workers came to him in the middle of an afternoon.

"We've got a problem. Melinda Erfer seems to be well enough physically to be discharged soon, don't you agree? However, emotionally she is still fragile and needs some long-term psychological counseling. She refuses to go back to the circus and I don't blame her under the circumstances. Her father and she haven't seen each other in years and she has no other relatives other than a sixteen-year-old brother and some distant cousins that she doesn't even have an address for. What do I do with her?"

George had been thinking some of the same things lately. Melinda had recovered physically but there were no places to put persons with her kind of problems. She wasn't eligible for one of the private sanitariums. Some people had kindly con-tributed money when the story first broke in the news and there was a small fund available for needy persons donated by the hospital auxiliary, but it would take much more for the six months or so that George estimated it would take for Melinda to regain her psychological balance.

"I don't know," he bluntly told the social worker. "Let me talk to my brother, Matt. Maybe in California they have some kind of program she could take advantage of. They seem to be much more progressive than here."

"You know how they begin to bug us about opening up beds. See if you can sew it up by the end of the week."

It was almost midnight when George finally got Matt's line. It took a long time to explain all the details. Matt was accustomed to consulting with George on difficult patients.

This time he could see the underlying emotions were putting a skewed aspect on the problem.

"Seems like you've gotten pretty attached to Melinda," he finally commented. "Why should I go out on a limb for this kid? It sounds like she did have it pretty rough but you're not only asking me to try to get her into a program but to house her with us for a while. We're brothers and all that but isn't this above and beyond?"

"Hell man, I think I'm falling in love with her. All this time and no romantic involvements! Said it could wait until I was all done and making money but these past two weeks have put all that resolve out the window. It's not that she's an interesting patient. I care more and more as I spend more and more time with her. I find so many things I like about her. Her spunk, her intellect, her sweet nature despite a horrible childhood. At first, I thought it was just pity but it's a lot deeper than that. Please help. You'd love her."

For the first time George was verbalizing his feelings, which were so intense he was amazed to hear himself saying what was in his heart.

"Could you bring her out so we could make a better judgment? At least, on the first weekend you're free, you could take a quick fly-out and back. If I'm convinced, she could work out here. In the meantime, I'll try to get her accepted in an experimental program we're running in Monterey. It's a live-in facility that they've just started for abused women. I'll call you back on Sunday."

"Wait until you meet her! We'll come out on the first weekend I'm free. And be prepared to take her because I'm buying her a one way ticket," George replied.

"Boy, you have it bad. I hope she's all you say she is and what will you do if we say no?"

"That's just it. I wouldn't be asking if I had any place else because it is going to be hard enough to have her so far away even for a little time until I'm out of here. Once I'm out there I'll assume the responsibility."

"I'm still going to call you Sunday. Calm down. I think I can work things out but it will take some time. At least it will be good to see you."

12

The Confrontation

The evening sun was near the horizon, and although the sky had begun to look as though it might rain, Melinda still stood by her window in the Adams Tower and stared across the sky-line of Sacramento. She was dimly aware that the lights should be turned on in her darkening office. She didn't want any light. She didn't want to return to the pages she'd been reading. Was it only an hour ago that the sunlight streamed in and Harry Jamison came in and presented her with this thick file?

"You're going to enjoy this one!" Harry gleefully chor-tled. "We finally have a big one, mob and all, to go to the grand jury. It will be just what you need for the upcoming election. Read it and enjoy. Let me know in the morning. I've got the wheels working already. Need your go ahead and we should be able to hold a press conference tomorrow in time to hit the six o'clock news. The feds have this one sewn up good and proper."

Thoughts flew through her head. Memories flooded in, unwanted and sharply real. She shuddered involuntarily and finally turned and sank into one of the comfortable 'visitors' chairs across from her desk where the open file rested. Never in her years of law had she come across such a perfectly designed, surefire case. Fraud, misuse of funds, money laun-dering, the works. If only it didn't involve her father. Was he as guilty as the paper trail seemed to lead? Why had she not paid more attention to his rise in the business world? After all, he was right here in California. And the strange way this had all been unearthed. To think Esmirelda was still able to cause trouble!

Melinda shuddered again as she thought of those years Esmirelda had interfered with her returning to live with her father. Now she knew the truth. That was one of the benefits of going to college and law school. She had managed to search all the old records and find out why she'd been placed in foster home after foster home. Now that she had reunited with her brother Richard they both knew where the blame lay. It was Esmirelda every time who had put a stumbling block to reunification of the family.

By instinct she reached for the phone to call George. Then she remembered. Darling, beloved George was in Switzerland attending a medical convention. Even Dell, her twelve-year-old, was away at summer camp. No one was home to notify that she was going to be very late for dinner. There wasn't any shoulder to cry on or ear to borrow with this problem which seemed to be lurking like a dragon. What could she do? Every instinct made her want to call her father and shout, "Tell me it is all lies!"

Her hand automatically reached up to smooth her hair, which she wore in a bun. She had started this hair style when she had wanted to look older when she had first joined the District Attorney's staff six years ago. Now that she was running for his job it made her look professional on the campaign posters. As she brushed her cheek she found it was wet. She looked down at her summer suit and saw that although she'd been unaware of it, she must have been crying for a while, for her blouse had a large wet mark on the front.

Melinda reached for the tissue box that at times had been helpful for clients, but she had never used. It had been many years, not since George had entered her life that she had shed tears. She had cried a lot when he proposed. *She had been in love with him since those first days in the hospital.* She had sublimated all the old hurts connected with her childhood and now a flood gate had opened. Sobs that began to shake her body couldn't be held back any longer. Self-pity for the years without her father and the miserable foster homes she'd experienced flashed in her brain. The final rape in the circus truck which she had tried to forget now became her father's fault. Or was it Es's fault? Or was it Rose's?

The sobbing continued well past dark. The office was now pitch black and as Melinda quieted and became aware of the dark, she automatically reached for the desk lamp. She rose from the chair and went into her private powder room to repair the damage to her face. Her eyes were red and puffy. Her blouse a damp mess. She was in no condition to go home to the housekeeper's questions. Better call and tell her to go home for the day, that she would eat out.

Before leaving the office, Melinda carefully placed the offending file in her bottom desk drawer. She would have to think about this overnight but didn't want to take the file home for fear that in anger she might destroy it. The night watchman didn't seem to notice when she signed out of the building. She often worked nights but hoped he wouldn't notice her mottled face. She walked to the parking lot and got into her BMW. It had been a gift from George when they'd celebrated their tenth wedding anniversary.

Flipping through her datebook she noted she was due at a brunch the following morning. Damn, now she'd not have much time to quelch Steve Mern's enthusiasm for a press conference tomorrow afternoon. It would take longer than that to fully explore not only how she felt but how many facts in the file could be corroborated.

What a poor time to have to make a solitary decision.

George was always so helpful in sorting out both sides of issues.

Her house had all the outside floods bathing the cool stucco walls in a rosy glow. It was a large house in the western section of Sacramento. Too big for just the three of them, but when George had been made head of neurology at the hospital they had to entertain frequently. Now there were numerous political gatherings. The house provided a handsome setting in which to host parties. The spacious yard and pool were ideal for informal meetings and get togethers.

Melinda sat, admiring the house for a few minutes before she pushed the button to open the garage doors. The connecting door to the family room was dimly lit and she proceeded through it to the kitchen where Grace, the housekeeper, had placed a tray for her with salad, sandwich and a thermos. How had she guessed that Melinda was lying about eating out? Or was the tray ready before she'd called and Grace had left in a hurry? In the rush of a busy day, Melinda had skipped lunch and now she was truly hungry.

As she munched away, a plan began to form. *Suppose it could be managed to slant the case in Es's direction?* Perhaps the facts could be a reflection of a sinister involvement that Esmirelda brought from her first husband's unsavory business dealings. *If only my father had gotten rid of Es way back when she'd been abusing me.* The facts in the file seemed to indicate that she was the one who had triggered the initial investigation.

Even though this was a federal case, the grand jury would take place in Sacramento. If Melinda had a press conference about the impending grand jury, she decided that perhaps she could cast doubt on the original motivation that had opened the investigation into her father's business dealings. Since the F.B.I. had already done such an exhaustive search and, from the look of the file, unearthed so much incriminating evidence, there was no way she could stop the case from proceeding. When would her conflict of interest come to light?

It was up to the Feds to announce the calling for the grand jury investigation, but by them sharing the file with her, Melinda felt they had given the go ahead for her to announce. *Did they know something of her connection with Douglas?* George had reassured her years ago after they first got married that even though her name was changed, that a first-class detective would be able to find out where she was. Instinctively she knew this and although her heartbreak of her father's having ignored her all these years hadn't surfaced for a long time, the desire for her father to try a reconciliation lay subconsciously behind her drive to succeed. If she could make him especially proud of her accomplishments, he might be more eager to establish a new relationship.

Richard didn't have the same desire to make up with their father. The last he remembered seeing him was when he was settling in at his one and only foster home. Richard considered them his parents and couldn't understand Melinda's motivation. Melinda hesitated to call to tell Richard about the upcoming grand jury and their father's probably being involved.

She had to talk to someone. Someone who would understand not only her reluctance to announce the fact at a press conference but who knew of her estrangement with her father. George was the only person to whom she had told all her story. Even though his brother and wife knew some of the facts, Melinda felt embarrassed to reveal that it seemed as though her father was a criminal and was being accused of extremely serious ties with the mob.

In the back of her mind Melinda kept denying that this was what the facts revealed. *There must be some mistake.* Or was her childhood memory of her father clouded with what had happened in the intervening years? The only solution was to call George and ask for his advice. There must be some excuse she could use to postpone the press announcement. Of course, since it would be a marvelous boost to her campaign, her committee would be very pleased that such a big case would be taking place and that she had been given the opportunity of announcing it. The big question was if anyone could find out that she was Douglas' daughter.

It was now almost nine o'clock. That meant that it was five A.M. in Switzerland. *Too early to call George?* Melinda decided to wait until ten. Frequently George got up at six when he had surgery. She sat at her desk in the upstairs den and pulled out a yellow legal pad. She started to write, as nearly as she remembered, the facts from the file.

It helped to write. First she outlined the facts. The F.B.I. had concrete evidence that the bookkeeper at the eastern plant had been manipulating the books. They had traced her connection with the mob and money laundering. In addition they had uncovered some connection with her father's prison friend, Horse. Horse had retired from business but his son, a lawyer who had connections with the mob, was running the eastern division of the large conglomerate. Charmain had met and was engaged to this son.

Melinda, who had never liked her stepsister, was sure that Charmain was just as vindictive as she had been when they were both in first grade. Melinda stopped writing. She began picturing the sequence of events that weren't in the file. She could imagine Charmain informing her mother of her intended's connection with the mob. Not knowing how it might hurt her daughter, Es had run to the F.B.I. with the information and also filed for divorce at the same time. What made Melinda smile at this point was that Es was still stupid about ramifications. The wedding was still being planned, Melinda could bet.

Theoretically, there should be no possibility of the press unearthing Melinda's connection to her father. Only if someone in New York was aggressive in digging into Doug's past would her connection come to light. Melinda knew that a case of this magnitude would have national exposure. On the one hand, this meant she would probably have her picture circulated nationally, which would be good for her campaign locally. On the other, there was a possibility that someone might recognize her and mention it to the press. Mrs. Erfer might be able to. Melinda doubted she would say anything to anyone. Then there were all the circus people.

Melinda got up, walked into the bath, and stared at the reflection. There was no hiding her distinctive eyes and the fact she was over six feet tall. Her hair was darker and worn in a different style but she had to admit that there was enough resemblance of herself at thirty-five to the teenager she was when she'd been with the circus. Suddenly she felt vulnerable. All along she'd thought of being exposed as Douglas' daughter only as a threat to her political career. It would be more far-reaching than events in the next few months would reveal.

"I'm acting unreasonably," Melinda told herself. "Time to phone George and get some input from him."

The phone rang seven times before George sleepily answered, "I told you I wanted to sleep late this morning. Call me at ten." With this he slammed down the phone.

Melinda tried again and before he had a chance to say a word yelled, "Help!"

At this, George sat on the edge of the bed and from habit began to dress. "What's the matter?" he asked in German.

"It's me, Melinda, darling. I'm sorry to wake you but I'm in the middle of a mess here and need your ear for a few minutes."

She began reading from the legal pad after she explained about the press conference. George was accustomed to her methodical approach to solving problems. When she finished, he sat and didn't answer for several minutes.

"I know you've been geared up to run for District Attorney, but perhaps you should put all that on the back burner for a while. It isn't that I think your link to your father would be exposed but you are too close to all of this to risk the chance. Why don't you use the press conference to announce your withdrawal from the race and let the Feds announce the grand jury investigation? You could say pressing family business has caused you to make this decision. It may be a good time to plan for another addition to the family. We could work on that as soon as I get home. You have lots of time to run for office after we have that boy we've always talked about."